RIDE ON, SISTER VINCENT

DYAN SHELDON

WALKER BOOKS
AND SUBSIDIARIES
LONDON · BOSTON · SYDNEY

For Sue

First published 1994 by Walker Books Ltd
87 Vauxhall Walk, London SE11 5HJ

This edition published 1995

2 4 6 8 10 9 7 5 3

Text © 1994 Dyan Sheldon
Cover illustration © 1994 Sue Heap

This book has been typeset in Sabon.

Printed in England

British Library Cataloguing in Publication Data
A catalogue record for this book is available from
the British Library.

ISBN 0-7445-3694-4

CONTENTS

THE LAST
OF ITS KIND

The rain slapped against the windows of St Agnes in the Pasture and the wind rattled the tiles on the roof. Like background music, water leaked through the ceiling into the old aluminium bucket in one corner of the kitchen in a steady *plop, plop, plop*. But no one at the large and sagging wooden table was paying any attention to these sounds. Mother Margaret Aloysius was saying grace.

" … and thank You, too, for that unexpected sunshine this afternoon," she was saying in the soft, formal voice she used when she was speaking to God. "It did give the kitchen roof a chance to dry out a bit, although of course that isn't to say that we aren't appreciative of the benefits of so much rain, especially when it comes to Sister Francis's garden…"

Helen Robbins cautiously opened one eye. There were two reasons why meals at the convent school of St Agnes in the Pasture were something of a trial, and one of them was Mother Margaret Aloysius' saying of grace. Although Helen was quite sure that God would be satisfied with a brief but sincere "Thank You, Lord", Mother Margaret Aloysius believed that He needed a detailed listing of every single thing they had to be grateful for since the last time they ate. Helen held back a sigh. At St Agnes, what Mother Margaret Aloysius believed was the way things were.

Still cautious, Helen glanced around her. Like Helen, the four nuns and the other two girls at the table had their heads solemnly bowed. Unlike Helen, they also had both their eyes closed, although Sara Mantawa, on Helen's left, was ruthlessly picking at a scab on her knee and Isobel Macauley, on her right, was scratching her ankle with the heel of her shoe.

" … and so we thank You, too, for sharing with us the bounty of Your earth, and especially for the meal Sister Francis has so lovingly prepared for us of which we are about to partake," Mother Margaret Aloysius summed up. "Amen."

"Amen."

"Amen."

"Amen."

"Amen."

"Amen."

"Amen."

The others, with the exception of Sister Germaine, all opened their eyes. Sister Simon began to serve the chicken and Sister Francis started passing the vegetables.

"Just wait till you taste the carrots," said Sister Francis, trying to sound enthusiastic. "They've got a special ingredient today."

Sara stared at the bowl of bright orange carrots swamped in what looked like muddy green string, and then she glanced at Helen. "Dandelion," she mouthed silently. Dandelion was Sister Francis's favourite secret ingredient; her second-favourite was nettles.

Sister Francis flapped her napkin. "And do try the nasturtium sauce, girls," she urged. "It's a new recipe from my herbal magazine. I'm sure you're going to like it." Helen was sure that she wasn't. She looked over at Sara and, raising her napkin to hide her face, pretended to gag. The second reason meals at St Agnes in the Pasture were something of a trial was Sister Francis's cooking. Mother Margaret Aloysius believed that Sister Francis should do the cooking because she taught science and tended the garden. Unfortunately, though Sister Francis tried to be bright and positive about her meals, Sister Francis was as interested in cooking as a rosebush is in plumbing – and as good at it.

9

"A new recipe," said Isobel, politely if unenthusiastically. "That's great."

Sister Germaine, the deputy head of the school, had been dozing peacefully through most of the Reverend Mother's prayer, but she now woke up suddenly. "New?" she asked. "Did someone say new?" She blinked at the other nuns. "Are we talking about the new Sister?"

"Bread?" asked Sister Simon, glancing warily towards Mother Margaret Aloysius. She picked up the basket of bread and almost hurled it in Sister Germaine's direction.

Ever obedient, Sister Germaine helped herself to a slice. "It will be nice to have a new face at the convent, won't it?" she asked brightly.

Isobel and Sara both glanced at Helen, but Helen was staring at Sister Germaine with unconcealed surprise. If life at St Agnes had any disadvantages besides the Reverend Mother's long graces and Sister Francis's cooking, it was the fact that nothing ever happened. It was Helen's opinion that nothing much had happened at St Agnes in the last hundred years.

She gave Sara a kick. Sara was the Reverend Mother's favourite student, which meant that she could get away with things that Helen and Isobel couldn't. Like asking questions.

Sara turned to Mother Margaret Aloysius with a politely interested expression on her face. "Oh, are we getting a new teacher?" she asked, sounding as though she didn't really care one way or the other.

"I'm afraid Sister Germaine is a little confused," said Mother Margaret Aloysius stiffly. She thrust the boat of nasturtium sauce at her deputy head. "It is true that we're being sent a new Sister, but we never asked for one. It's a mistake."

Sister Simon nodded. "A computer error."

"Exactly." Mother Margaret Aloysius pursed her lips. "A computer error."

Mother Margaret Aloysius didn't like computers. She didn't like anything she considered too "modern", like television, videos, Hollywood films, or fax or answering machines either, but most of all she didn't like computers. She blamed them for most of what she considered wrong with the world – which was a great deal.

Isobel, weary of trying to scrape the dandelion from her carrots, looked up. "But if we're getting a new teacher..." she began timidly.

Mother Margaret Aloysius glared at her darkly. "If we're getting a new teacher what?"

Isobel stared into Mother Margaret Aloysius' clear blue eyes like a rabbit caught in a car's headlamps. "Well, it's j-j-just... I r-r-reckoned..."

Mother Aloysius stabbed at her chicken.

"Do stop stammering, Isobel, and tell me what it is you reckoned."

Helen exchanged a look with Sara. Mother Margaret Aloysius had recently decided that it was time to shut down St Agnes. Mother Margaret Aloysius was tired. Sister Francis, Sister Germaine and Sister Simon were tired, too. They weren't as young as they used to be, said Mother Margaret Aloysius. It was time for a rest. The nuns had dedicated their lives to St Agnes, but keeping the school going had become an uphill struggle. Enrolment had been dropping steadily for a decade, and since the new comprehensive opened the year before, the last of the day girls had gone. Now the only pupils in the school were Helen, Isobel and Sara. Both the Mother General and the Bishop had suggested that modernization would solve the school's problems. If St Agnes "joined the twentieth century", as the Bishop put it, it could attract students, staff and funds. But the Reverend Mother wouldn't hear of it. As far as she was concerned, St Agnes wasn't about swimming pools, computers and hamburgers and chips. It was about history, tradition and values. St Agnes had been run on certain principles for over two hundred years and it would continue to be run that way, or not at all.

Helen could tell that Isobel was hoping that the arrival of a new teacher meant that Mother

Margaret Aloysius had changed her mind. Life at St Agnes was boring, and the food might be awful, but that didn't mean that they wanted to leave. As Sara often said, "Better the nuns you know than the nuns you don't know."

"I-I-I…" Isobel was going from pink to red in a rather alarming way.

Helen went to her rescue. "If we're getting a new teacher, then doesn't it mean that St Agnes won't be closing at the end of term after all?" she blurted out.

Everyone looked at Helen, especially the Reverend Mother.

"No, Helen," said Mother Margaret Aloysius coldly. "That is not what it means. All it means is that there's been a mistake. We didn't ask for new staff, and we certainly don't need any. Sister Germaine, Sister Francis and Sister Simon and I shall be retiring as planned and you girls shall be going elsewhere."

"B-b-but—" bleated Isobel.

"But nothing," said Mother Margaret Aloysius. "My mind is made up. Perhaps times have changed, but that doesn't mean that St Agnes must change. St Agnes stands for something—"

The crashing of an upstairs shutter into the courtyard obliterated the end of her sentence.

"It won't be standing long at this rate," whispered Sara.

ONE OF A KIND

The bus lurched around a bend, and Sister Vincent's head hit the rain-splattered window. "Welcome to the countryside," she muttered to herself. The bus hit another rut.

Straightening out her wimple, Sister Vincent glanced round the bus. The driver had assured her that this was, indeed, the Friday bus to Little Anstis, but Sister Vincent was beginning to wonder if he'd misheard her. Except for the fat man with the duck in a box, who was sitting behind her, the few other passengers from the train who had got on with her had all got off what seemed like hours ago. Sister Vincent and the man with the duck had earlier had a brief conversation about the annual county show, the problems of journeying with live fowl, and the advantages of raising llamas, but at the moment both the man and the duck seemed to be snoring.

Sister Vincent looked out of the window with a sigh. Aside from the storm, there wasn't anything to see.

"Cows," Sister Vincent said softly. "Sheep. Horses. Fields." She sighed again. They were so far from anywhere Sister Vincent considered civilization that she might as well be in the Australian bush. "As You know, Lord," she went on, "I am a great admirer of Your handiwork, and I have nothing against nature *per se*, but I am a city girl. I do feel a lot more comfortable with concrete and cars than with grass and large animals with teeth."

In answer, the Lord cut the sky with a razor of lightning.

Sister Vincent leaned back in her seat. "I know," she said. "I shouldn't question, I'm Your tool. I should trust."

Sister Vincent had always trusted in the Lord, and He had always proved most trustworthy. Wasn't He always directing her to places where she could be most useful? Hadn't He sent her to Lima to help those abandoned children? Hadn't He sent her to Los Angeles to help that street gang? Hadn't He sent her to London to help those refugees? And hadn't He been right to send her? "I do trust," Sister Vincent continued. "You know I do. It's not that I'm questioning Your methods, it's just that…" Her words trailed off.

It was just that, this time, she was being sent

not to a violent inner city or a troubled third-world capital, but to a convent school set in the middle of a meadow. No one in Sister Vincent's last posting had ever heard of St Agnes in the Pasture. They couldn't even find it on the map. It seemed to Sister Vincent that the only problem St Agnes could have was that everyone had forgotten it. What possible use could the Lord have for her there?

The bus bounced in and out of a series of ruts and then came to a sudden stop. Sister Vincent peered through the glass. She could just make out a post office and a grocer's shop. Her fellow passenger had woken and was putting on his mac. The duck was quacking. The driver left the bus.

Sister Vincent turned round. "Excuse me," she said to the man with the duck. "Excuse me, sir, but where are we now?"

He looked over. "End of the line, Sister." He put on his canvas hat, he picked up his duck, and he started down the aisle.

"Little Anstis. Last stop."

At least she was on the right bus after all. "Oh, no," said Sister Vincent, "I believe there's one more stop."

Her travelling companion started to squeeze past her seat. "Really?" he said. "One more stop?"

Sister Vincent nodded. "Yes," she said. "This bus also goes to St Agnes in the Pasture."

17

Both the man and the duck looked puzzled. "Saint what?"

"St Agnes in the Pasture. I believe it's a few miles from the village."

"St Agnes..." The duck still looked puzzled, but the man nodded slowly. "That's right," he said. "There was some sort of convent in the valley."

"Is," Sister Vincent corrected him.

"Is?" He gave her a rueful smile. "Are you sure, Sister? I had the impression that it closed down years ago."

Sister Vincent's answering smile was rueful as well. She was beginning to wonder just how small St Agnes's really was. It was one thing for no one in London to have heard of it. And perhaps in Big Anstis, assuming there was a Big Anstis, St Agnes might have escaped everyone's attention. But she would have thought that the people of Little Anstis would know it was still there.

"It's a school," she explained. "A convent school." Included with her orders had been a prospectus for St Agnes. Sister Vincent tried to remember what it said. "It was built in the farmland surrounding Little Anstis nearly two hundred years ago," she informed him, "and it's one of the largest and most progressive schools of its kind."

"Really?" said the owner of the duck. "But I don't remember seeing any St Agnes girls at the county fair in recent years. Are you sure it hasn't shut down?"

"Of course I'm sure," said Sister Vincent. She dragged out one last piece of information. "The school motto is 'Creativity, not conformity; thought, not recitation'."

Her companion didn't look too impressed by this. "It just goes to show you how deceptive appearances can be, doesn't it?" he asked with a laugh. "Here I was thinking it was just some empty old buildings, and in fact it's one of the biggest schools in the country." With some difficulty, given the smallness of the aisle, the largeness of himself and the quacking of the duck, he fished inside his mac pocket and pulled out a damp rectangle of heavy paper on which was printed GUNGA DIN DUCK FARM. "Here's my card, Sister. Drop by if you're ever in Lower Smeaton. Maybe your convent needs some poultry."

Maybe my convent does need some poultry, thought Sister Vincent as she slipped the card into the pocket of her jacket and watched him lumber towards the exit. It probably needs poultry more than it needs a mechanic.

The driver got back on board. "Just fifteen more minutes, Sister, if the bridge isn't washed away," he called to her.

"And if it is?" she asked as the doors closed and the engine turned over.

19

The driver met her eyes in the rearview mirror. "Probably no more than a day," he answered cheerfully.

For just a second it occurred to Sister Vincent that she should turn right round and go back to London. After all, if the bridge had washed away and the storm continued, she might have to wait days before she got to the convent. Surely no one would expect her to do that, would they? The engine groaned in a pointedly disgruntled way. Apparently someone would.

Sister Vincent smiled back at the driver. "Only a day?" she said. "Well, that's not too bad, is it?"

The rain stopped as the bus returned to the road.

"St Agnes, last stop!" called the driver as they bounced to a stop on a deserted hilltop.

Sister Vincent stood up, peering through the windows. Except for the remains of an ancient stone wall, all she could see was a wood. "Where?" she asked.

The driver opened the door and stood up. "Down there," he said, pointing through a clump of trees. "I'm afraid the road's bad and the hill's too much for this old bus, or I'd take you down."

"I'm sure I'll manage," said Sister Vincent with a glance at the sky. She picked up her luggage – a blue and yellow satchel and a large black metal box – and walked down the aisle. When she reached the front she stopped behind the driver. "I still can't see anything," she said, peering round him.

"Oh, it's down there," he assured her. "At least it was last time I came up here."

"And when was that?" she asked hopefully. Perhaps not everyone had forgotten St Agnes. Perhaps the Friday bus stopped here every week.

He shrugged. "Maybe last year," he said, frowning thoughtfully. "Maybe the year before."

I knew I shouldn't have asked, Sister Vincent told herself. She readjusted her luggage.

The driver turned, reaching towards the box. "Here, let me help you, Sister."

"Oh, no, thank you very much, but I'm fine," said Sister Vincent. "I'm afraid it's rather heavy."

"Heavy?" The driver laughed. "I think I can handle it," he said with a wink as he grabbed the box from her hand. There was a frozen second in which no one spoke and nothing moved, and then the driver gave a strangled cry and hurtled down the steps, still desperately clutching the black metal box as he landed in a hedge.

"What have you got in there, Sister? Bibles?"

"Oh, no, not Bibles." Sister Vincent picked up her box and smiled at him. "Tools."

She could feel him staring after her as she walked away. If past experience was anything to go by, he was probably wondering what kind of nun she was.

Slinging her satchel over her shoulder and tucking the box under her arm, Sister Vincent started humming a rock 'n' roll tune under her breath.

Although the bus driver couldn't know it, of course, as far as nuns went, Sister Vincent Euphrasia was one of a kind.

FIRST IMPRESSIONS AREN'T ALWAYS THE BEST

Sister Vincent's first sight of St Agnes in the Pasture was not inspirational.

"That's not it, is it?" she asked as she came to the top of the lane and looked down at the dark grey buildings across the valley. The convent looked slightly like the drawing in the prospectus, if you assumed that the drawing had been done quite a long time ago, before the buildings started to collapse.

A thick drizzle began to fall.

Sister Vincent put down her luggage and pushed her glasses up on her forehead. She squinted through the weather. She gave the long, low whistle she'd learned on the streets of L.A.

"Good glory..." she whispered. No wonder the man on the bus had thought that the school had been closed. "I can see that it must have been quite attractive eighty or ninety years ago," said Sister Vincent, slowly. "But it is falling down now, Lord." She shielded her eyes with her hand. Not only did the convent have an abandoned air, but there was nothing around it for as far as the eye could see. "You are sure it is still open, aren't You?" she added gently.

A sudden wind shook the tree tops.

She looked up. "It doesn't seem a bit on the deserted side to You?" she inquired.

The drizzle turned to rain. She squinted a little harder. "No, no, I beg Your pardon," she said, pulling her glasses back in place. "You're absolutely right. I do see some lights in the main building." There were also quite a few chickens huddled under the bushes by the front door. "And chickens. Low-watt bulbs and bantams." More chickens than lights, she supposed.

"I was right," said Sister Vincent. "St Agnes does have more use for poultry than for a mechanic."

She looked upwards as an unexpected fist of lightning turned the sky pink and purple.

Sister Vincent picked up her luggage. "I know, I know," she said as she started down the lane. "More action; less talk."

The wind blew across the hilltop again, and the trees Sister Vincent was passing under drenched her with water. She adjusted the hood of her anorak. It wasn't always easy being an instrument of the Lord.

From their point of view, Helen's, Sara's and Isobel's first sight of Sister Vincent wasn't much more inspirational than her first sight of St Agnes. She was splashing up the driveway, mud splattered over her orange anorak and silver wellies, a blue and yellow satchel slung over one shoulder and a large black box under her arm. Helen could make out travel stickers on the satchel and the box, but she was too far away to see what they were. The new nun looked to Helen like someone in disguise.

"That can't be her," said Isobel as the small, sodden figure marched determinedly up the drive. "She doesn't look anything like a nun." Isobel swiped at her glasses with the corner of her jumper.

Helen popped a chocolate into her mouth. "It has to be her," she mumbled, her eyes still on the peculiar figure approaching the house. She could just make out a damp wimple crushed under the bright orange hood of the anorak. "Nobody else ever comes here but the postman. And she doesn't look much like him either."

Isobel frowned, a sign that she was thinking. "But she isn't dressed right," she persisted. "Her glasses are pink! And she isn't even wearing black."

"You've spent too much time at St Agnes,

Izzy," said Sara. Her eyes didn't move from the window, but she shook her head and the beads on the ends of her plaits clicked. "Not all nuns wear long black habits. The only reason the sisters here do is because Mother Margaret doesn't want to be modern."

Helen rested her chin on her arms, dribbling chocolate crumbs. "And anyway," said Helen, "if she wore a black habit she'd never get her anorak over it."

This time, Isobel tried removing her glasses to clean them. "I still say she doesn't look like a nun. She doesn't even walk like a nun. She walks like she's hiking."

Sara leaned out into the rain as the new Sister started up the front steps. "It's a long way from where the bus drops you, and there is a lot of mud," she said logically. "Besides, lots of nuns go hiking. I even heard Mother Margaret Aloysius say she once went hiking in Europe."

"Nuns don't hike in silver wellies," argued Isobel. "And they don't wear anoraks either."

"Nuns who come from London do," said Sara casually, glancing over at her friends to check their reaction to this new piece of information.

Helen reacted immediately. "How do you know she comes from London?" she demanded. Much to Helen's annoyance, Sara always managed to find out what was going on before she did. Sara claimed this was because she was more sensitive and intuitive, but Helen reckoned it was because Sara was so much nosier.

"I just happened to overhear Sister Germaine and Sister Simon talking about her after breakfast, that's all."

"Oh, of course…" Helen smiled sarcastically. "And I don't suppose you happened to overhear what the name of the nun from London is, by any chance?"

Sara smiled back serenely. "Sister Vincent."

Helen poked her. "Come on," she ordered. "What else did you overhear?" It might annoy her that Sara always knew more than she did, but at least Sara couldn't keep a secret.

"Not much, really." Sara shrugged. "Sister Germaine said that Sister Vincent's transfer was all very irregular. She said they hadn't even been sent her real records, but that she seems to move around a lot. She said that Mother Margaret Aloysius threw a wobbly when she got the letter saying Sister Vincent was coming, but that when she rang the Mother General's office they wouldn't cancel the transfer."

Isobel was still watching Sister Vincent standing on the porch in the rain. "It's not just the goggles and all that stuff," she was muttering to herself. "There's something strange about her. She looks too young or something."

Helen drew back from the window as Sister Vincent finally disappeared through the front door. "You've definitely been here too long, Izzy. Not every nun in the world is old, you know. It's only at St Agnes that they all remember the Second World War."

Sara leaned against the windowsill, her arms folded in front of her. "No, Isobel's right, there is something strange about her. But it's not that she's too young. It's something else…"

Helen threw herself on her bed, reaching under the pillow for another bar of chocolate. She wished the new nun would stay. A Sister in silver wellies with travel stickers on her luggage might liven things up. Helen sighed. "If she moves around a lot, that means she's restless. Which means she's going to hate it here. She won't last more than a day and a half, she'll find it so boring."

"You don't know that," argued Isobel. "We find it boring here, but we still like it."

Helen tore the wrapper from the chocolate. "That's because we're used to it," she said.

"It doesn't matter," cut in Sara. "If Mother Margaret Aloysius doesn't want her to stay, then it doesn't matter if she wants to or not." Helen nodded. At St Agnes in the Pasture, the Reverend Mother's word was law.

Isobel propped herself on one elbow, looking from Sara to Helen. "You never know,"

28

she reasoned. "Mother Margaret Aloysius might get to like her after all. She might change her mind."

Helen and Sara exchanged one of their "That's Isobel" looks. Despite a tendency to worry and fret, Isobel always made an effort to look on the bright side when she could. Helen found her forced optimism almost as annoying as Sara's skill as a spy.

"Izzy," said Helen, leaning over and patting her hand. "Izzy, if you remember, Mother Margaret Aloysius nearly went mad when the doctor said Sister Germaine should wear trainers for her bunions. She went on as though he'd said Sister Germaine should wear high heels. She's not going to be really keen on a Sister who wears an anorak and wellies."

"And besides," said Sara. "Mother Margaret Aloysius never changes her mind." She threw herself into the only armchair in the small room. "If Mother Margaret Aloysius were capable of changing her mind, then we wouldn't have to leave St Agnes at the end of the year."

"Don't," ordered Isobel. She put her hands to her ears. "I don't want to hear it."

"It's going to happen whether you hear it or not," said Sara. "And, besides, maybe it won't be so awful. Change can be a good thing, can't it, Helen?" She didn't sound too convinced.

"That's true," Helen agreed quickly. "Change can be a good thing." She didn't sound too convinced either, even to herself. But Isobel, she was relieved to discover, seemed to believe them.

"It's all right for you two," she said sulkily. "You have parents and homes. I'm the one who's the orphan. St Agnes is the only home I've ever had."

Helen stopped chewing. "I don't have parents and I don't have a home," she said flatly, trying not to remember the time when she did have parents and a home. "I have a father and I have a list of poste restantes." Helen had come to St Agnes two years ago, after her mother died, because her father, a photographer, travelled so much that he couldn't look after her.

Sara shook her head in agreement. "I'm not much better, you know. When do I ever see my parents? I never go home and they never visit." Sara's parents were botanists who spent most of their time in remote areas looking for rare plants. Isobel's optimism wavered; she sniffed back a tear. She really couldn't bear the thought of leaving the school. Life at St Agnes might be boring, and it might be dull, but the school was her home and the Sisters and Helen and Sara were her family. She was even fond of Mother Margaret Aloysius when she wasn't terrified out of her wits.

"But aren't you upset that St Agnes is going to close down?" asked Isobel. "Won't you miss it?"

"Of course I'm upset," said Helen, who didn't really want to admit, even to herself, just how upset she was. "If I go to a different school, my father will never remember the new address and I won't even get a postcard now and then." Helen frowned at her chocolate bar. The truth was that even though St Agnes was unexciting she, too, was miserable at the thought of leaving. It wasn't just Isobel's home, it was hers as well. If it hadn't been for the nuns and Sara and Isobel, she might never have got through those first awful months after her mother's death.

"And I'll miss it, too," said Sara. "But there's nothing we can do about it. We just have to accept things as they are."

Helen looked over at Sara. Sara, she decided, wasn't admitting how much leaving St Agnes would upset her too. But then, Sara was used to accepting things as they were. She'd had to be. She'd been in boarding schools for as long as she could remember, and she'd always felt lonely and out of place. As strange as St Agnes was if you were used to television and videos and normal food, she'd told Helen that it wasn't until she came here that she knew what it was like to have a real home. For the first time in her life she felt as though she belonged.

31

Sara had also told Helen that she should have known it was too good to last.

Helen tossed her chocolate wrapper into the bin. "If only Mother Margaret Aloysius weren't so stubborn..." she mused.

Isobel wiped another tear away. "If only some more pupils would come to St Agnes..."

"If, if, if..." snapped Sara. "Wishing doesn't make things happen."

Downstairs, doors were slamming. The three girls listened. Sister Germaine's trainers could be heard scurrying down the hallway to the Reverend Mother's study. "The new teacher's arrrived!" she was calling. "Sister Vincent's here!"

"What's the use of *ifs*?" asked Sara glumly. "It would take a miracle to save St Agnes now."

THE LORD WORKS
IN MYSTERIOUS WAYS

Sister Vincent had hoped that her impression of St Agnes might improve upon closer inspection. But as she sloshed up the lane leading to the convent, she realized that her hope had been misplaced. Everything about the house sagged or tilted or drooped. Even the grounds around it looked tired. The closer she got to St Agnes, the clearer it was that its charms were few and its character was doubtful.

Sister Vincent came to a stop on the broken drive. A small yellow bulb by the front door flickered over the several grumpy chickens huddled on the porch. "They obviously don't have a lot of visitors," she commented ironically. "Those chickens probably haven't moved in years." The Lord, however, wasn't in the mood for irony. The porch light went out completely.

Aware that she had said the wrong thing

again, Sister Vincent put on a more positive, if not exactly enthusiastic, smile. "I'm sure it's much better inside," she commented loudly as she climbed the stone steps. "Cosy and homely." She stepped carefully over the dozing chickens. "Welcoming." A sudden gust of wind blew rain in her face. She pushed the bell.

Sister Vincent spent several nervous minutes waiting to be pecked on the ankle by a disgruntled chicken before she realized that the bell didn't seem to be working. She put her ear to the old wooden door and rang once more. Not only couldn't she hear the bell, she couldn't hear anything else either. It was so quiet inside that if she hadn't seen those three faces watching her from an upstairs window, she might have thought that everyone was out. With the resolution of a woman who once disarmed a gunman in Lima with a lug wrench, Sister Vincent grabbed hold of the knocker and whacked it soundly. Nothing. She whacked it again. Nothing. She was just about to whack it for the third time when the door suddenly opened with a groan.

A small, round nun in the long skirt and flowing veils of the traditional black habit stood smiling up at her. "Yes, my dear?" she asked, pleasant but puzzled. "What can I do for you?" Sister Vincent stared, at a rare loss for words. *Good glory, she doesn't even real-*

ize I'm a nun, she thought. "Progressive" didn't really seem like the right description of St Agnes. Progressive in the Stone Age, perhaps, but not at the end of the twentieth century. Not wanting another wave of rain in her face, she smiled cheerfully. "Sister Vincent," she said, extending her hand. The elderly nun blinked.

"Sister Vincent?" Her eyes travelled from the silver wellies to the neon-pink glasses, finally alighting on the crooked grey wimple poking out from under the orange hood. "Oh! Sister Vincent! Of course! Of course! We've been expecting you." She grabbed the extended hand. "I'm Sister Germaine," she went on, pumping Sister Vincent's arm. "I'm so sorry, I didn't rec— I thought you mus— Come in, come in. Mother Margaret Aloysius is waiting in her study."

Sister Germaine steered a bantam back through the front door with her foot. "Don't mind the chickens," she said. "Just shoo them out of your way."

Sister Vincent aimed a gentle kick at what she took to be a small grey hen, and promptly tripped over a bucket positioned under a leak in the roof. "Do be careful," warned Sister Germaine as she slowly led the way down a gloomy corridor to the Reverend Mother's study. "There's not too much light, I'm afraid. There's something wrong with the electrics."

That doesn't surprise me, thought Sister Vincent as she guided herself through the darkness by keeping one hand on the wall. It seemed likely that there was something wrong with everything here. "It's very quiet," she whispered as they walked along. "Is it evening prayers?"

"Oh, no, no, I'm afraid you've missed evening prayers," Sister Germaine called brightly over her shoulder. "The television's broken, and of course we don't usually put on the radio until *A Book at Bedtime.*"

Sister Vincent squinted ahead of her, trying to separate the nun from the shadows. "Oh, of course," she agreed. No television? No radio? Probably no cassette player or stereo. Nothing to listen to but the rain dripping through the holes in the roof.

Sister Germaine came to a sudden stop in front of a heavy mahogany door. She knocked.

"The new teacher's arrived!" she announced. "Sister Vincent's here!"

Sister Vincent was still worrying about the lack of television and radio. She would miss her favourite programmes. She wouldn't know what groups were at the top of the charts. She'd brought some of her favourite records with her, but it seemed unlikely that the convent would have anything to play them on. *At least I have my Walkman.* She was comforting herself as she ploughed into Sister Germaine, who was opening the study door. The two of them shot into the room, landing with cries of surprise only inches from the desk.

The Reverend Mother looked down on them. "I suppose this must be Sister Vincent," she said without any enthusiasm.

"At your service," said Sister Vincent, and she pulled her wimple out of her eyes.

"That'll be all for now, Sister Germaine," said Mother Margaret Aloysius.

Sister Vincent, standing now, smiled humbly, as befitted someone who had landed on the floor with her skirt around her knees.

Mother Margaret Aloysius did not smile back. Instead, she fussily arranged her black veils, folded her hands in front of her on her large wooden desk, and peered over her steel-rimmed spectacles at Sister Vincent with a stern expression.

Sister Vincent's smile became a little more humble. If anything, the Mother Superior's expression was even more stern now than it had been when the two nuns fell into the room. With a sinking feeling, she realized that a stern expression was probably the Reverend Mother's favourite.

"I'm very sorry that you've had this long journey for nothing, Sister," Mother Margaret Aloysius was saying in a voice without emotion. "But I'm afraid that the computer has made some sort of mistake." She paused to clear her throat. "As I told the Mother General when I first heard of your appointment," she went on, "I didn't ask for another nun, and I most certainly do not need one."

Sister Vincent couldn't help noticing that the Reverend Mother had no difficulty at all in keeping the sorrow she was feeling out of her voice. *Good Glory, I've been here only five minutes and already she doesn't like me.* She gave her wimple a tug to straighten it out, but said nothing. It was rapidly becoming harder, not easier, to understand why the Lord had brought her to St Agnes.

Mother Margaret Aloysius gazed down at the single sheet of paper in front of her. "And if I had asked for a nun," she continued in the same flat tones, "I most certainly wouldn't have asked for you." Her finger stabbed at a line of type halfway down the page. "'Motor mechanics,'" she read unhappily. Her eyes came back to Sister Vincent. "Motor mechanics?" she repeated. "I have never in my life heard of a nun who taught motor mechanics."

Sister Vincent could tell that some response was necessary, but she wasn't quite sure what. She glanced up at the ceiling as though expecting some help. The overhead light dimmed slightly. "Motor mechanics have come in very handy in my other postings," she explained. "Very, very handy." She smiled brightly. "You'd be surprised."

"I'm sure I would," said the Reverend Mother drily.

Sister Vincent continued as though Mother Margaret Aloysius had been encouraging. "Yes, indeed... Why, there was an incident in Peru—" She was about to launch into an account of how she had finally managed to save several small children from being sold on the black market in Lima only because she knew how to disable a car that would otherwise have been chasing her, but Mother Margaret Aloysius interrupted her.

"Peru," she said, sounding as though she'd just bitten into something sour. The light from her desk lamp glinted off the steel rims of her glasses. She scrutinized Sister Vincent's record again. "You certainly have moved around quite a bit."

Sister Vincent wasn't sure if the Reverend Mother seemed thoughtful or suspicious. "I go where the Lord calls me," she answered simply.

"Peru, California, Ireland, Africa... He seems to call you quite a lot." Mother Margaret Aloysius tapped slowly at the paper. "Everything about you is irregular, Sister Vincent." She frowned. "Your records aren't complete, no one at the Order's central office seems to know anything about you, and you don't stay very long in one place."

Sister Vincent gazed through the window at

the moon, just visible in the sky behind the Reverend Mother's head. A cloud slipped past the moon, making it look as though it were winking.

"There's a lot to be done," said Sister Vincent mildly.

"In the world, perhaps," replied Mother Margaret Aloysius. "But not at St Agnes." She took off her glasses and looked up at Sister Vincent again. "The Lord didn't call you here," she said firmly. "I'm quite sure that the computer called you here," she said. "The computer short-circuited, that's all." She smiled unenthusiastically. "There's nothing for you to do at St Agnes, Sister. We don't own a car. Not even a small one. And if we owned a dozen cars, it wouldn't matter. The school will be closing at the end of the term, so we really have no need of your services, do we?" It was more a statement than a question.

Sister Vincent, however, decided to treat it as a question. She straightened her wimple again, and nodded slowly, as though thinking this over.

"Well, I did see some of your pupils at the window as I arrived, Mother Margaret, and I must say that they looked like just the sort of girls I like to teach."

Mother Margaret Aloysius rose. "Those weren't some of our pupils," she said coolly. "Those were all of them."

Old-fashioned, falling down, no television, no radio, no stereo and no pupils. I'm beginning to wish I'd never left Peru. Sister Vincent smiled again. "Well, it is true, you know," she said out loud. "The Lord does work in mysterious ways."

"Not this mysterious," said Mother Margaret Aloysius.

SISTER VINCENT
AND ST AGNES
GET ACQUAINTED

Sister Vincent got out of bed on the wrong side
the next morning.

She blamed her bad mood on dinner. Dinner
the night before had been less than delight-
ful. The meal had been dull and full of
weeds. The other Sisters had been quiet and
withdrawn, except for Sister Germaine, who
slept through all of Grace and most of the
pudding. The pupils had been quiet and
withdrawn, except for Sara, who watched
her as though she were trying to memorize
every detail of Sister Vincent's face and
clothes. Mother Margaret Aloysius had also
been quiet and withdrawn, except when
she was glaring at Sister Vincent across the
mugwort sauce and mumbling about computers. On top of that, Sister Vincent had slept
badly because the mugwort sauce had
given her indigestion. And on top of that, a

demented cockerel had woken her before dawn.

"It's not that I don't like a challenge," Sister Vincent was telling the Lord now as she dressed. Dawn was finally breaking, and since she was already awake she'd decided to explore the convent before the others were up. Experience had taught her that a little snooping could go a long way. She might even discover why she was here. "I do like a challenge," she continued. "There's nothing I like more than a challenge, You know that." She pulled a woolly crimson jumper over her head. "Wasn't Los Angeles a challenge?" she whispered. "Wasn't London? And what about Lima?"

The Lord didn't answer.

Sister Vincent sighed. She was used to the Lord's silences. Sometimes He might shake a few trees or flicker the lights or make it rain a little harder to make sure she knew what His opinion was, but often He made no response at all.

Thinking of London, Sister Vincent looked around her. Her room in London had been large and airy and cornflower-blue. She'd kept a model of the internal combustion engine on the bureau, and from the large bay window she could see the Post Office Tower. The room she was in now was so small that she had to stoop to avoid hitting her head on the ceiling. She guessed that its walls had once been white.

The only thing on the dresser was a statue of St Joan with a sheep standing beside her.

"This isn't a challenge," Sister Vincent muttered as she reached for her wellies. "This is a test of endurance."

The Lord said nothing, but the harsh, grating sound that had woken her before sunrise started again. She looked out of the window. Instead of the rooftops of Hampstead and the Post Office Tower, she saw an overgrown courtyard, a weathered barn on the verge of collapse, and the cockerel who was making such a racket it was a wonder the whole county wasn't up. "I do think I'd prefer taking my chances with the street gangs of L.A.," Sister Vincent complained as she tugged on her boots. "At least they have sidewalks and takeaways in Los Angeles. And no cockerels." The crowing became a little more urgent.

"All right, all right," said Sister Vincent. She put on her glasses. "I'm on my way."

Helen had been having a wonderful dream until the crowing woke her up. In the dream, her father had come to St Agnes to visit her. He'd taken a photograph of her, Sara, Isobel and the nuns in front of the house. They'd all been smiling, even Mother Margaret Aloysius.

"Some day I'm going to strangle that chicken," she announced from under her pillow.

She heard Sara roll over. "It's not a chicken," Sara mumbled sleepily. "It's a cockerel."

"It's going to be a casserole with dandelion leaves if it doesn't shut up," said Helen. "I'll even help Sister Francis prepare it myself." Isobel's bed creaked as she sat up. "I can't sleep anyway," she informed them. "I'm too worried."

Helen didn't stir from under her pillow; Sara yanked the blankets over her head. The cockerel crowed more urgently.

"I can't sleep anyway," Isobel repeated, a little more loudly. "I'm too worried."

Helen groaned. "You're always worried about something," she muttered. "If it's not the ozone layer, it's whether or not there'll be biscuits for tea."

"I'm worried about leaving St Agnes." Isobel looked from the lump that was Sara to the lump that was Helen. "I really thought Sister Vincent might change things," she went on, undaunted by the fact that she was largely talking to herself. "Even though Mother Margaret Aloysius said it was all a mistake, I still hoped that everything would work out. But after what she said last night..." Isobel's words trailed off into a sigh.

Helen shut her eyes more tightly, trying to get back into the dream she'd been having. Not only had the Mother Superior introduced

46

Sister Vincent as a "visitor", but Sara had overheard her say that she was going to ring the bishop this morning and ask him to sort the problem out.

"Lie down, Izzy," ordered Sara. "You can worry when it's daylight."

"But I can't sleep," Isobel insisted. She climbed out of bed, wrapping a blanket around her shoulders for warmth. "You know I can't sleep when I'm worried like this."

Helen lifted one corner of her pillow, glaring at Isobel with her one opened eye. "And you know I can't sleep when you're pacing back and forth like that," she grumbled. It was at times like this that Helen wished they didn't have to share a room to save on the heating bill.

"Isobel!" Sara's head appeared from under the covers. "Get back to bed, will you? The sun's not up yet. You and that cockerel are the only ones who are."

Isobel stopped pacing, as though something had suddenly caught her attention. "No, we're not," she said. "Sister Vincent's up, too."

"Really?" asked Sara.

Helen emerged from under her pillow. She looked over at Sara. "I wonder what Sister Vincent's up to," said Helen.

"Me, too," said Sara, already starting to pull on her clothes.

* * *

"Ducks," said Sister Vincent, gingerly wading through a large puddle that had been left at the side of the house by yesterday's rains. "Ducks would definitely enjoy it here."

A tile loosened by yesterday's winds tumbled off the roof, landing at Sister Vincent's feet. "And a builder," she added. She stepped over the tile and squelched on, thinking about all the other things that St Agnes needed. An electrician. A television repairman. A troop of actors or at least a rock band until the television repairman came. Heat. Pupils. She glanced through the window of the dining-room as she passed. Much like the mugwort sauce, the memory of last night's supper returned. "Fun," she said aloud. "Fun and a cook who isn't quite so keen on weeds." Her mind still on the peculiar colour of the nettle pudding, Sister Vincent came round the side of the house and into the courtyard.

"Good glory!" she cried, stopping sharply. "Has Little Anstis been at war?" Behind her pink-framed glasses, her eyes moved around the yard; beneath her woolly crimson jumper her heart dropped like a berry in a bowl of milk.

For if the nun's house was run-down, then the only way to describe the rest of the convent was run over. The back fence was broken, and the chicken coop had lost a wall. Weeds grew between the cracks in the pavement and there was a hole in the roof of the barn big enough to throw a baby elephant through. The only building still intact was the school itself, but that had been boarded up and abandoned now that there were only the three girls left. In the shimmery morning light, everything had an air of defeat.

"A miracle," she whispered. "That's what St Agnes really needs. A miracle, not a motor mechanic." Sister Vincent looked skywards. "You'll excuse me, Lord," she said, carefully choosing her words so as not to offend. "You know that I don't like to tell You how to run Your business, but if You could just give me a hint about what's on Your mind…"

A calm, reasonable voice answered immediately. "Who are you talking to?" it asked. It was not the voice of the Lord.

Startled, Sister Vincent spun round. Sara Mantawa, Helen Robbins and Isobel Macauley were standing on the path behind her.

"What are you three doing skulking about so early?" she demanded.

"Izzy couldn't sleep," said Helen.

Isobel nodded. "I saw you leave the house."

Sara was looking round the courtyard as though expecting to see someone else. "We thought you might want us to show you around."

Sister Vincent looked down at her. She

couldn't decide what intrigued her more about Sara – her hairdo or her obvious talents as a secret agent.

"Oh, did you?"

"Uh huh." Helen pulled a rumpled white bag from her jacket and shoved a caramel into her mouth. "We reckoned that was why you were up so early. Because you were already bored."

Sister Vincent reached over and snatched the bag from Helen's hand. "No sweets before noon." She shoved it into the pocket of her skirt. "And why should I be bored?" she wanted to know. "An intelligent person is never bored, young lady. If you're bored it's because you're not doing enough."

"We're bored because there isn't anything to do," said Sara.

"Everybody at St Agnes is bored," Helen continued. Despite the fact that there was no one in the yard but the cockerel and a chicken or two, she lowered her voice. "I bet even Mother Margaret Aloysius is bored."

Sister Vincent made no comment. She bet that Helen was right.

"It wasn't always like this, though," said Isobel. "There used to be other pupils, and Sister Francis used to take us on field trips in the countryside."

"That's right," agreed Sara. The beads on her plaits shone like a rainbow in the sun.

"And Sister Simon always had us making things. She used to hang our paintings in the school hall."

"Even Sister Germaine used to be interesting," said Helen. "Before she started falling asleep in class all the time."

Isobel rubbed at her glasses with the sleeve of her jacket. "That's why we were hoping you were staying. We thought you might ... you know ... liven things up."

Sister Vincent pursed her lips. "Isobel Macauley, either clean those glasses properly or take them off," she ordered. "And for your information, I am a nun, not a TV entertainer." Her eyes shifted from one girl to the other. "And just what makes you think I'm not staying?" Isobel looked at Helen, who looked at Sara, who looked surprised.

"Mother Margaret Aloysius said so at supper," answered Isobel. "We all heard her. She said you were only visiting."

"Well, there are visits and there are visits," said Sister Vincent vaguely.

"And I heard her say she was going to talk to the bishop today," Sara blurted out. "To ask him to have you sent back to London."

Once more, Sister Vincent's eyes came to rest on Sara. "Oh, did you? You certainly have very good hearing."

Sara smiled as though accepting a compliment. "I happen to be very sensitive."

"You mean you happen to be very nosey," said Helen.

Isobel slipped her hand into Sister Vincent's. "What would you like to see first?" she asked. "The chicken coop? Sister Francis's garden?"

A small but mischievous smile appeared on Sister Vincent's lips. "You do make it sound very exciting," she said.

Helen giggled. "We can go inside and see the really boring things like the laundry room and Sister Simon's potting wheel later."

A sudden burst of sunlight drew Sister Vincent's attention across the courtyard. "What about the barn?" she asked. "What's in there?"

"Nothing," said Helen.

"Nothing," Isobel echoed.

"Some mouldy old newspapers and a few chickens," said Sara.

Welcome to St Agnes in the Pasture! Sister Vincent brushed her hands on her skirt. *Although, if you ask me, it's more like St Agnes in the Cowpat!* "Then perhaps we ought to start somewhere else." She absent-mindedly reached into her pocket and removed one of Helen's sweets. She put it in her mouth, and wondered once again what she was doing here. A cloud scudded across the sun.

THE DARKNESS
THAT COMES BEFORE
THE DAWN

"Here at St Agnes we take great pride in doing things the way we've always done them," said Mother Margaret Aloysius icily.

"Well, nobody else does," answered the bishop. "The rest of the world has moved on, Mother Margaret. The rest of the world has discovered the microchip and cable TV."

"Don't talk to me about microchips," snapped the Reverend Mother. "It's a faulty microchip that's put this motor mechanic in hiking boots on my staff." A chip of paint as large as a fifty pence piece floated down from the ceiling, past her eyes, and onto the desk. Mother Margaret Aloysius sighed. She was tired of paint flaking off the ceilings. She was tired of tiles falling off the roof. She was tired of the leaks and draughts and faulty wiring that plagued the house.

"You blame progress for everything," the

bishop was saying. "But the simple truth, Reverend Mother, is that you and your staff are relics of the past."

"I thought the Church believed in relics," Mother Margaret Aloysius commented wryly.

The bishop paid no attention. "If you'd listened to me years ago," he rolled on, "you wouldn't be down to three pupils whose parents are too lazy to move them."

"Too lazy!" cried the Reverend Mother. "Laziness has nothing to do with it. Sara Mantawa's parents respect Sister Francis's botanical knowledge. And Helen's father—"

"Helen's father has always been too busy even to visit the school," thundered the bishop. "And all of that is beside the point, Mother Margaret. The point is that pupils would have flocked to St Agnes if you had computers and videos, if you fed them frozen food and organized dances and made sure that they memorized what every other school child in the country was memorizing…"

Mother Margaret Aloysius moved the telephone a few inches from her ear. She was also tired of the bishop banging on about technology and the twentieth century.

"Our motto has always been 'Creativity, not conformity; thought, not reci—' "

The bishop cut her off. "We are all in favour of thinking," he assured her. "But if you don't mind my saying so, Mother Margaret, your problem has always been that you can't tell the difference between compromise and conformity."

The Reverend Mother most certainly did mind his saying so. She shut her eyes. She especially minded as it was something he'd said so often in the past. "Oh, really?"

"Yes, really. This time, however, I'm afraid that you're finally going to have to compromise whether you like it or not."

The sharp blue eyes snapped open. "Meaning?"

There was a sound much like that of a cat scratching at the carpet, which Mother Margaret Aloysius rightly interpreted as the bishop clearing his throat. This was not a good sign.

"Meaning that I can see no reason for sending Sister Vincent back to London now. She can leave when the rest of you leave at the end of the year."

"But she's not supposed to be here," argued Mother Margaret Aloysius. "She's a mistake. A computer error. Surely if you had a word with the Mother General—"

Once more, the bishop cut her off. "I'm afraid the other phone is ringing, Mother Margaret. I'll have to go now. We'll let you know when the committee will visit to decide what to do with St Agnes after you're gone."

Mother Margaret Aloysius sat for a few seconds, listening to the dial tone and staring at the crucifix on the wall. "After you're gone!" she muttered to herself. He made it sound as if she were going to play the harp in heaven not to retire in Cornwall.

Deep in her heart, Mother Margaret Aloysius suspected that the bishop was right. *She* was what had gone wrong with St Agnes. Somewhere along the line she'd lost her fight and spirit. She'd struggled for so long against cutbacks and dwindling enrolments and changing times – but in the end she'd had to admit to herself that the world no longer wanted what St Agnes had to offer. The new comprehensive had been the last straw. How could they hope to compete with a heated pool, computer networks, modern science labs, and hamburgers and chips for lunch? Why should they try? That was why she'd decided to retire; she didn't have the energy to fight anymore. Retirement might be a form of surrender, but it wasn't the same as giving in.

Mother Margaret Aloysius leaned back in her chair. "St Agnes will end as it began," she said, swiveling round to face the window. "With a dedication to history and tradition." Through the mullioned glass she caught a glimpse of Sister Vincent disappearing through the back door. "And with a motor mechanic," she added with a sigh.

Meanwhile, Sister Vincent was trying to find

out why she'd been brought to St Agnes. That was why she'd decided to talk to the other members of her new community, to see if they could give her any clues. Talking to Sister Germaine, however, was not as easy as it might sound.

"So you teach English, history and knitting," Sister Vincent prompted. Sister Germaine, sitting across from her in the armchair, snored gently.

Sister Vincent sighed. There were several things that she believed in with all her heart. The first was the Lord. "Trust in the Lord," Sister Vincent always said, "and even if your feet get wet, you'll know you're on the right path." From the Lord came the other things she believed in, such as love and goodness, hope and joy. She also believed that the darkest hour was just before the dawn. She had spent the morning trooping around the convent with Isobel, Sara and Helen – from the chicken coop to the fuse box in the cellar – looking for some glimmer of light that would explain her presence at St Agnes, and so far it was still as dark as the inside of a crankcase. Sister Vincent leaned forward and tapped Sister Germaine on the knee.

The old nun opened her eyes in surprise. "Don't tell me I dozed off again?"

Sister Vincent's eyes fell on the statue of St Brigid with a sheep peering out from behind her on the shelf above Sister Germaine's head.

Sister Germaine sighed. "It's these scarves," she said, taking up her knitting again. "I used to help the girls put on plays and musicals in my spare time, but now that there are only the three, I knit. It's a little ... you know ..." she lowered her voice to a whisper, "repetitious, knitting beige scarf after beige scarf, day after day."

Sister Vincent looked from Sister Germaine to the laundry basket filled with identical scarves at her side. "Perhaps you could use some different colours," she suggested. "I'm sure the poor wouldn't mind."

Sister Germaine leaned towards Sister Vincent conspiratorially. She lowered her voice. "Can I tell you a little secret?" she asked.

Before Sister Vincent had a chance to reply, she went on. "I don't actually knit these for the poor anymore," said Sister Germaine, her voice barely a whisper. "It's really just to give me something to do. I used to knit for the poor, you understand, but the poor have had enough. They want T-shirts with pictures and slogans on them, not scarves."

Sister Vincent looked at the coils of beige wool. She couldn't decide which they reminded her of more: draft excluders or scouring pads. She could see the poor's point. She'd much prefer a T-shirt that said I, THE INTERNAL COMBUSTION ENGINE herself.

"Well, then," she said brightly. "Why not throw in a little pink, for instance, or a bit of purple or yellow, just for yourself?"

Sister Germaine's needles clicked rhythmically. "We got the beige wool cheap in a job lot," she explained.

"You could dye the wool," Sister Vincent suggested. "Sister Frances must have a lot of herbs and plants that are natural dyes. You could try some of them."

Sister Germaine shook her head. "Oh, no, no," she said quickly. "Mother Margaret Aloysius wouldn't approve." Her voice got even lower. "The Reverend Mother doesn't really approve of bright colours, you see. I think she associates them with pop music."

"Pop music?"

"Pop music and telly advertisements." Sister Germaine's eyes went from Sister Vincent's deep red jumper to the neon-orange laces on her trainers. "Mother Margaret Aloysius blames them for a lot of the ills of the world."

"Them and computers..." murmured Sister Vincent, her own eyes moving to the left to avoid joining Sister Germaine in staring at her glowing laces. A smiling statue of St Angela, a small sheep asleep at her feet, looked back. Saints Bartholomea and Vicentia, a sheep between them, were on the windowsill behind Angela.

"Not that it really matters," said Sister

Germaine, abruptly returning to scarves. She shook her head sadly. "I shall have to stop soon, anyway. I'm running out of places to store them."

"Um…" said Sister Vincent. She felt that the topic of scarves had pretty much been exhausted. What she really wanted to talk about was the Reverend Mother.

"Mother Margaret Aloysius doesn't really seem to approve of very much," she said. And then, thinking that might sound a bit uncharitable, hastily added, "Very much that's modern."

"I'm afraid most of us get a little conservative as we get older," said Sister Germaine. Her eyes went to the ceiling. "But when I first came here, I was just back from Africa and St Agnes was even more exciting than that had been."

"Africa?" Sister Vincent didn't try to hide her surprise. She'd assumed that Sister Germaine had always been at St Agnes. At least that explained who plaited Sara Mantawa's hair.

"Africa…" repeated Sister Germaine in a faraway voice. "Now there's a place for colours… Colours … sounds … smells…" Her voice trailed off as she leaned back, seeing things Sister Vincent couldn't see. "You should've seen Mother Margaret Aloysius when I first arrived, Sister," she finally went on. "You wouldn't have recognized her. She was so spirited ... so bold. The pupils didn't just learn things, they lived them. When we did Julius Caesar they were Romans. When we studied World War II they re-enacted the Blitz in the basement. Why, Mother Margaret Aloysius once organized the girls in a demonstration against fox hunting in Upper Smeaton." Sister Germaine smiled to herself at the memory. "Believe me, Sister Vincent, this school used to throb with energy and laughter and imagination…"

"What happened?" The question was out before Sister Vincent could stop herself. She glanced upwards as the ceiling light dimmed. When she looked back, Sister Germaine was sound asleep.

"You must be running out of saints by now," said Sister Vincent, her eyes darting round the pottery studio. According to her estimate, there was at least one statue of a saint in every room of the convent, including the bathrooms and the downstairs w.c. Hundreds of others seemed to be stored here. There was obviously as little demand for Sister Simon's statues as there was for Sister Germaine's scarves.

"Some of them are repeats," said Sister Simon. She was as tall as Sister Germaine was short, as thin as Sister Germaine was fat, and as untidy as Sister Germaine was neat. She slapped at the clay in front of her, causing a fine red mist to drift across the table.

"I take it that's Saint Margaret you're doing now," said Sister Vincent, trying to dodge out of the way of the spray.

Sister Simon's clear brown eyes looked into Sister Vincent's face with unconcealed curiosity. "How did you know that?"

Sister Vincent coughed, her eyes on the ground. "She's wearing a monk's habit."

Sister Simon laughed. "Well, you're better at identifying the saints than I am, I must say." She turned to her again, holding one clay-covered finger to her lips. "Don't tell Mother Margaret, will you, but I just make the faces up as I go. As long as I have the clothes right and maybe a bit of local scenery…"

"And a sheep," said Sister Vincent, flicking a bit of clay from her jumper. It was amazing how quickly Sister Simon had managed to get clay not only on her hands, her apron, her face, and in her hair, but everywhere else as well.

Sister Simon winked. "You noticed the sheep, did you?"

Sister Vincent cast another glance at the hundreds of tiny faces staring back at her from the shelves around the room. Noticed them! How could she have missed them!

A warm, contented smile had settled on Sister Simon's face. "Can you keep a secret?"

she asked.

Sister Vincent nodded. "I can try."

"I love sheep," Sister Simon announced with real affection. "I grew up with them. Times come and go, but sheep are always with us." She sighed. "That's why I came to St Agnes in the first place. Because it was in the country." She lowered her voice. "And that's why I started the pottery. I wanted to share my love with the world." She smiled at Saint Margaret. "Why, I made sheep dishes and sheep planters ... sheep bowls, flower pots and lamps... You name it, and I could turn it into a sheep."

Sister Vincent leaned a little nearer, but not so near that she was likely to get any more clay on her. "But, Sister Simon, you don't really make sheep. You make saints."

Sister Simon flipped her veil over her shoulder, leaving two red fingerprints on the black cloth. "Mother Margaret Aloysius didn't approve of the sheep," she said, still whispering.

"She thought they were too modern?" asked Sister Vincent.

The red fingerprints shook. "Oh, no. Too frivolous. She didn't think making sheep was a good example for the girls." Sister Simon sighed. "A lot of the girls were very keen on pottery back then. Very keen. We were even planning to build a fountain of dancing sheep in the courtyard." Sister Simon started working again. Clay sprayed over her like mist. "The saints were the Reverend Mother's idea. To give me something to do when the day girls left. She thought Sara, Isobel and Helen would benefit from depictions of the great female saints. You know, that it would inspire them."

"And has it?" asked Sister Vincent.

"Has it what?"

"Inspired them."

"I shouldn't think so." She looked over. "Unlike you, I don't really think they know who they're all supposed to be." Her stubby hands poked and prodded the clay. "Not that one can blame them. I'd be surprised if even you could recognize St Brigid, or Saint Vincentia, or Mildred or Jane."

Sister Vincent cleared her throat. "Well... I might hazard a guess at one or two of them..."

"Really?" This time Sister Simon's look was more than curious. "Just what is it Mother Margaret Aloysius said you teach again?" she asked.

"Motor mechanics," said Sister Vincent.

Sister Simon stared at her. "Really? I would have guessed your subject was Religion."

Sister Vincent gave her a big smile. "What about sheep stools?" she asked. "Have you ever thought of making them?"

"Cookery? Oh, I wouldn't want to teach

cookery." Sister Francis looked horrified at the suggestion. "I hate cooking. Always have. When I was a girl I liked to tinker around the house – you know, put up a shelf here, mend a wire there – but I never, ever liked cooking. Perhaps I should have been a boy."

Sister Vincent fought back a smile. She had no trouble picturing Sister Francis, who was taller than Sister Simon but built like an American football player, as a boy.

"I just meant that as you do so much of it," Sister Vincent explained, though it rather relieved her to learn that Sister Francis disliked cooking so much. She'd have hated to think that she was so bad at something she loved. "Of course your real passion is for science, not food."

"It's not for science, either," said Sister Francis simply. She shook her head. "I suppose it's a sign of age, but though I still teach science, I'm not really as keen on it as I used to be." She shrugged philosophically. "All those quarks and leptons and interferons... It's hard for an old lady like me to keep up. What I used to love best was tinkering with things. You know, finding out what made them work. I used to teach the girls to make their own crystal sets." She smiled and suddenly looked years younger. "We even used to do a project where we ran electricity into the Wendy House. Of course, that was before it fell down." She waved one hand. "But these are my great love now," she said, indicating the mobs of dried herbs and flowers hanging from the ceiling. "They're not exactly modern, but they do keep me busy."

Sister Vincent stood in the middle of the kitchen, trying to keep a look of polite interest on her face as something brown and feathery chased something white and feathery over her feet. "I can see that they must," she said, stepping back with a cry of alarm into a small bush suspended from a beam. "You have so many of them," she said, glancing uneasily behind her. The kitchen of the convent in Peru had featured small reptiles and some rather large insects, but she had expected that sort of thing there. Peru was a third-world country. What she hadn't expected was chickens and shrubbery in a kitchen in Little Anstis.

"It's amazing how much you can do with herbs," said Sister Francis.

"Amazing," murmured Sister Vincent, finally able to take in the shelves and counters crammed with crocks and pots now that the chickens were out of the way.

Sister Francis beamed at her. "I like to think of my garden as my pharmacy," she said. "Mine and God's."

More like your jungle, thought Sister Vincent, who had fought her way through Sister Francis's garden and felt she knew what she was talking about. She jumped as something dead but sharp tried to dislodge her wimple. Sister Francis opened a large cupboard, revealing packed rows of neatly labelled jars and bottles. "And now that there isn't so much teaching to do, I've had a lot of time to experiment, of course." She undid the lid of a jar containing a greenish liquid and held it out. The odour of old gym socks filled the air.

"Good glory—" said Sister Vincent, trying not to gasp. These were gym socks that had been sitting in a damp cupboard for some time. "And what is that for?"

"Car-sickness."

"Car-sickness?" For the first time since her arrival, Sister Vincent felt that she really was about to discover why she was here. "You mean there is a car after all?"

"Car?" Sister Francis blinked in bewilderment. "No, no, we don't have a car. Not since the engine fell out of the Mini." She reached for another bottle that smelled unpleasant and held that out, too. "But then we don't have anyone with the gout here either," she said.

Sister Vincent became thoughtful. "Just what do you do with all your plants and herbs and teas and tinctures?" she asked. "You can't possibly use that much here."

"Well, I have had my little successes, if I do say so myself. I cured Sister Germaine's lumbago, and Isobel's catarrh, and Mother

Margaret's asthma last spring. Aside from those, though…" Sister Francis's voice trailed off. She looked at Sister Vincent. "Are you any good at keeping a secret?"

"I'm getting better," said Sister Vincent.

Sister Francis leaned close, her voice low. "I know it's very wasteful, but I have to throw most of my concoctions away." She spread her hands in any empty gesture. "What else can I do? There's nowhere to keep them."

"Perhaps if you put up a notice in the newsagent's in the village. I'm sure a lot of people would be interested in—"

"Oh, no!" Sister Francis looked shocked. "People aren't interested in old-fashioned remedies anymore. They want pain-killers and laser surgery."

Sister Vincent was about to say that Sister Francis might be surprised, but she didn't get the chance.

"And besides," whispered Sister Francis. "Mother Margaret Aloysius wouldn't approve. She doesn't like advertising, you know."

"So I heard," said Sister Vincent. She kept her smile on Sister Francis as she added to herself, *Mother Margaret Aloysius doesn't like much!*

A clump of comfrey fell on her head.

Rain swept across the courtyard, seeped through the cracks in the house, and dripped through the roof. Sister Vincent leaned against the window of her tiny bedroom, looking out into the night.

"There's really only one conclusion to be drawn here," she was saying conversationally. "And that's that Mother Margaret Aloysius is right and there really was a computer error." The plain cotton curtain fluttered in the draught. "But what else can I think?" she asked. "Scarves, sheep, herbal remedies… What can I do with scarves, sheep and dried twigs?"

Something clattered to the ground outside.

"You heard how resigned everyone sounds. You've seen how tired the Reverend Mother looks. How can I help people who don't want to be helped?" A deep, low rumble, which might have been thunder, rolled across the convent.

"But there's no reason for me to be here," argued Sister Vincent. "They don't even have a car. How can I help when they don't even have—"

A sudden wash of lightning illuminated one corner of the yard. Sister Vincent stared at the barn, standing out against the darkness like a star for one frozen second.

"The barn?" whispered Sister Vincent, but it wasn't a question. It might not yet be dawn, but at least she had seen a flash of light.

DAWN TAKES
A STRANGE FORM

The barn door creaked open slowly, and a slender figure dressed in an anorak, flannel pyjamas and wellies entered cautiously. The strong beam of a heavy-duty torch cut through the blackness, revealing dark, ghostly shapes in every direction.

"So that was the darkest hour, and this is the dawn," said Sister Vincent, almost instantly starting to cough. "Good glory," she gasped, choking on the dust and the rather pungent aroma that seemed to come from every corner of the barn. "Bat pooh." She clapped a hand across her mouth and nose. "And cat pee, rodent droppings, wood rot and mould," she added as she took a few more steps forward. "It's like being inside a peat bog."

As her eyes gradually adjusted to the lack of light, she moved the torch steadily around the room. The ghostly shapes turned out to be several old wardrobes, bureaus and bedsteads, a rusted tractor and a broken baler, scores of cardboard boxes and dozens of stacks of decaying newspapers. A disappointed sigh drifted through the gloom. Sister Vincent had rushed out here in her bed clothes in the middle of the night because she'd been hoping to find the old Mini that Sister Francis had mentioned in the barn, or even an ancient van from the days when the school was large and prospering. She hadn't expected it to be filled with cast-off furniture and useless farm machinery. She'd expected it to contain some sign that she was in the right place after all, not the makings of a jumble sale.

Sister Vincent let the torch linger on the ancient tractor. The headlamps were gone. Some dawn. "Good glory!" cried Sister Vincent, jumping as something scuttled between her feet and then ducking as something else swooped over her head. Rain streamed down on her from cracks in the roof. "I suppose I should have waited till the morning," she mumbled as she tried to move out of the way of the leaks and tripped over something solid. "But patience has never been my strongest virtue," she added, picking herself up and straightening her wimple. A clap of thunder sounded over the barn. "I'll work on it," she promised. "I will work on it." She pointed the torch towards the ground.

Several seconds passed while the rain splashed on the floor and small creatures scampered into the corners and fluttered in the eaves – and Sister Vincent stared down at the object she'd tripped over with a mingled look of disbelief and excitement. It was a tyre. It was worn bald and extremely filthy, but it was a nineteen-inch studded Avon nonetheless. Neither a Mini nor a tractor took a nineteen-inch studded Avon.

Sister Vincent slowly raised her head. "Where is it?" she whispered. There was a nervous twitter above her, but otherwise the barn was silent. "It must be here somewhere," she mused, spinning the light once around the room. "But where?" Holding the torch up in front of her, Sister Vincent began moving carefully through the barn. She peered into boxes. Some of them were filled with beige wool scarves; some with saintly statues; some with jars and bags of herbs.

"It's lucky this barn is here," mumbled Sister Vincent. "Or there wouldn't be any room for furniture in the house." Something small and dark glided past her head.

Sister Vincent abandoned the boxes. She climbed into wardrobes. She checked behind the smallest pieces of furniture. She even pulled up the cover on an old settee and looked under that. Nothing; nothing that required a wheel. "Please don't let there be any rats waiting to jump at me," she prayed as she crouched under a wooden wagon. The torch light fell on a two-legged stool, a heap of Sunday papers and a startled mouse.

Mindful of the broken rungs of a ladder, she climbed to the loft. "And if You don't mind, Lord, I know they're Your creatures, too, but I'm not really overly fond of spiders. Not in the dark." The torch light uncovered a bottomless pail, a crooked pitchfork, and a small city of boxes, but nothing that might fit a nineteen-inch Avon tyre. "I definitely should have waited till the morning," Sister Vincent said as, defeated, she backed down the ladder. "But I do mean it, I will try to be more patient in the future. I really wi—" Her voice broke off as her foot slipped and the torch fell from her hand, hurtling towards the hillocks of newspaper below. It was a few seconds before she realized that the sound the torch made when it landed was not the sound of a silver torch thudding against soggy paper, but the sound of a silver torch hitting something metal.

As soon as it was light enough the next morning, Sister Vincent tiptoed back to the barn to resume her search for the fallen torch – and whatever it was the torch had fallen on. "There is something here, isn't there?" Sister Vincent asked as she set to work. "I know there is. All I need is a little time by myself—"

but her words were cut short by the sound of the barn door creaking open.

"We've had an idea, Sister Vincent," said a voice behind her.

Sister Vincent, absorbed in breaking down the wall of newspapers to one side of the barn, didn't turn round. She didn't have to; she recognized the voice immediately. It was muffled because Helen had something in her mouth. "What time of day is this to be eating chocolate, Helen Robbins?" she demanded.

"It's not chocolate, it's jelly beans," said Helen.

"Actually, it was my idea," said Isobel softly.

"Jelly beans?" grunted Sister Vincent, pulling free a large bundle of papers in a cloud of dust. "What sort of an idea is that?"

Sara sneezed. "Not jelly beans, Sister. Giving us lessons."

"Bless you," said Sister Vincent, coughing a little herself as she heaved another stack to the floor. "Lessons in what?"

Helen chewed. "In geography. Sister Germaine says you've travelled a lot. Sara's parents are in Indonesia and my dad's in Brazil."

"And I've always wanted to go somewhere," said Isobel.

"Well, I *have* been somewhere," said Sister Vincent, "but that doesn't mean that I give lessons in geography." She grabbed hold of another bundle with a sigh. Helen popped more jelly beans into her mouth, crunching softly. "It wasn't my idea," she protested. "It was Isobel's. She thought it would give you something to do."

"I have something to do," said Sister Vincent as the third load of papers crashed to the ground. "And I was doing it quite well before you three decided to interrupt me." She straightened up quickly, for the first time catching sight of something not covered with newsprint.

"That's not true, Helen," Isobel was protesting. "I thought it would give *us* something to do, too, and you know it. You're the one who said you thought it was a good idea."

"Exactly what are you doing, Sister Vincent?" asked Sara.

Sister Vincent turned slowly round.

The three girls stared at her, so surprised by what they saw that Helen even stopped chewing. Isobel's eyes were on Sister Vincent's grease-stained grey dungarees. Sara's were on Sister Vincent's name, embroidered in red over her dungarees pocket. Helen's eyes were on the pink bandana tied across Sister Vincent's nose and mouth.

"What are the three of you gawping at?" asked Sister Vincent.

"You look like a train robber," said Helen,

breaking the slightly stunned silence.

"Don't be ridiculous," said Sister Vincent. She dusted her hands on the front of her uniform. "I look like no such thing."

"I knew you'd be bored here," said Sara.

Sister Vincent sighed loudly. "How many times do I have to tell you, Sara? An intelligent person is never bored."

"So what are you doing, Sister Vincent?" asked Isobel.

"What does it look like I'm doing? I'm looking for something."

Helen rolled a jelly bean between her lips in a reflective manner. A thin red line trickled down her chin. "And what are you looking for?" she asked.

Sister Vincent turned to where Helen was pointing behind her. Just peeping over a stack of papers was a set of handlebars. "That," she said, with a triumphant smile, "is what I was looking for."

Isobel frowned. "A lawn mower?"

Sara gave an exasperated sigh. "Your glasses must be dirty again, Izzy. That isn't a lawn mower. It's some sort of bicycle."

Sister Vincent didn't explain. "Helen," she said, "if you look to your left you will see a bucket, some rags and a torch. Please pass me the torch. But be careful of your hands, don't get it all sticky."

Helen started to argue, but the dungareed

figure was leaning over the bundles of papers again, so she picked up the torch as she'd been told and went over to Sister Vincent. The torch beam shone off something that might be silver.

"You see," said Isobel. "It is a lawn mower. You can tell by the shape of the handlebars."

"You're blind as a geranium," said Sara, squeezing forward. "It's definitely a bicycle."

"Funny bike," mumbled Helen. "Maybe it's some sort of pram."

The morning sun glinted through a ragged hole above them. "You're all wrong," said Sister Vincent. As soon as she'd heard the torch hit it last night, she'd known it was there, buried under rubbish, but she hadn't known what kind it would be. Now she did. "Of course, the headlamp's missing, so it's hard to tell," she went on, "but that, young ladies, is a motorcycle." The girls pressed forward, standing on tiptoe. There, indeed, was a large, clapped-out-looking motorcycle, brown with dust and rust.

"I told you it was a bike," said Sara, leaning so far forward she would have pitched over the stack of papers if Sister Vincent hadn't hauled her back by her jumper.

"But who could have left a motorcycle here?" asked Helen.

Sister Vincent seemed to consider this. "I wonder…"

Helen popped another sweet into her mouth. "Whatever it's doing here, it doesn't really matter, does it?" said Helen. "It's just a piece of junk. That bike's so old it's amazing it has wheels."

"A thing isn't worthless just because it's old, Helen," said Sister Vincent, heaving herself over the barricade to get a closer look. "Sometimes the old things are the best."

Sara climbed up on the papers to get a closer look. "Not if they don't work they're not," she said.

Sister Vincent straightened her wimple. "Then I'll just have to make it work, won't I?"

"What happens after you get it fixed?" asked Helen, licking sugar from her fingers.

"Then the bike will work," said Sister Vincent. She took up her bandana and began dusting off the seat.

"And then what?" persisted Sara.

"Then I should think I'll be able to take it for rides," said Sister Vincent impatiently. She started wiping the body of the bike.

Beneath the deep layer of dirt on the tank, the name VINCENT appeared in white lettering on a gold background.

"But that's your name!" cried Isobel. "Look, Sister Vincent! That's your name!"

Sister Vincent was rubbing off more dirt. "I can read, you know, Isobel," she said over her shoulder. "It's a Vincent Black Shadow."

But Isobel was suddenly excited. "Don't you see?" she demanded, looking from Sara to Helen. "It's from God."

Sara and Helen looked back.

"You really have been here too long, Izzy," said Helen, "if you think that God's given us His motorcycle. Can you picture Mother Margaret Aloysius on a bike?"

"Wouldn't it make more sense if He gave us something practical?" asked Sara. "Like a van? Or even a heated pool?"

Only Sister Vincent, intent on rubbing the grime from the motorcycle, didn't look at Isobel.

"No, you don't understand." Isobel scrambled up beside Sara, her words tumbling out in a rush. "He didn't give it to us to ride! He gave it to us because it's an antique. It's probably worth a fortune. God gave it to us so we can sell it for thousands of pounds, and then Mother Margaret Aloysius will change her mind about shutting down St Agnes and she'll use the money to do up the school, and we won't have to leave after all!"

"Where do you get these ideas, Isobel?" Sister Vincent was looking at her now, her expression one of concern. "God does not just hand people easy solutions, you know. God helps those who help themselves."

"And anyway," said Helen, "even if God did give us the motorcycle, Mother Margaret

Aloysius isn't going to like it."

"Don't talk with your mouth full, Helen," snapped Sister Vincent.

Helen became indignant. "All I said was—"

Sister Vincent, gazing into space, started talking over her. "You know," she said, "I haven't felt this excited since that time in Lima when I was chased through the back streets with a car full of orphans."

Sara looked at her. "When were you in Lima, Sister?" she asked.

"Before I went to Los Angeles." She smiled at the memory. "Of course, that was rather exciting, too."

"Lima… Los Angeles… No wonder you're bored here," said Helen.

"How many times do I have to tell you, Helen?" asked Sister Vincent without turning around. "An intelligent person is never bored."

Helen was about to answer, "Are you sure about that, Sister Vincent?" but she didn't have the chance.

"Yes, Helen," said Sister Vincent, lovingly patting the seat of the motorcycle. "Yes, I'm absolutely sure."

GOD HELPS
THOSE WHO HELP
THEMSELVES

Sara decided to spend the afternoon washing the bathroom window. It wasn't the way she usually spent her free time. Usually she spent it doing nothing, but today the fancy had taken her to do a little window washing. Even Isobel seemed surprised. "You? Volunteer for a chore?"

"The Sisters are so old," said Sara compassionately. "I do like to help them out when I can."

"No, you don't," said Helen. She licked chocolate from her fingers. "You just want to keep an eye on the courtyard, in case something happens with Sister Vincent's motorcycle."

"I don't know why you always doubt my motives," said Sara stiffly. Without another word, she marched out of the room in a huff, banging her bucket against the doorframe.

Helen was writing a letter to her father. Normally, Helen didn't have very much to tell her father, but today the words were just pouring onto the page. She was just describing finding the Vincent Black Shadow when Sara burst into the room.

"Quick!" Sara shouted. "I just saw Sister Vincent and the Reverend Mother going towards the barn. I bet she's told her about the motorcycle. They're going to look at it now!"

Helen raised her head from the page. "Are you sure?" she asked cautiously, but she was already putting down her pen. If Sister Vincent and Mother Margaret Aloysius were going to have an argument about the bike, Helen didn't want to miss it.

Sara caught her breath. "Of course I'm sure. I just saw them come out of the kitchen."

Helen couldn't resist a swipe at Sara. "What a coincidence," she said. "It's a good thing you decided to take up housework today after all."

"I'm going to ignore that remark." Sara grabbed her jacket from the chair. "Come on, we have to hurry if we don't want to miss too much."

Isobel, who'd been lying on her bed, staring at the ceiling, suddenly looked over. "Miss too much of what?" she asked. She sounded puzzled.

Helen groaned. Sometimes she really wondered what Isobel would do without her and Sara to explain things and guide her.

"Miss too much of what Mother Margaret Aloysius says to Sister Vincent when she sees the motorcycle," said Helen.

"But the Reverend Mother isn't going to let us listen to their conversation," Isobel said, frowning. "You know what she's like."

Sara stopped in the doorway. "For heaven's sake, Izzy. We're not going into the barn. We're just taking a walk."

"Near the barn," added Helen, and the two of them vanished into the hall.

"May the angels pray for us, I thought that was a camel coming down the stairs!"

At the sound of Sister Germaine's voice, Helen stopped dead just as she was about to jump the last two steps. She'd gone back for her bag of fruit gums and had been hurrying to catch up with Sara and Isobel, but now she watched in horror as the side door banged shut behind them and Sister Germaine emerged from the shadows. "Helen?"

Helen turned. Sister Germaine had several scarves around her neck and a patient but curious look on her face.

"Did you hear me?" she asked. "Where are you three off to as though the devil himself were at your heels? I haven't seen you girls move that fast since the television blew up."

"Us?"

"Is there anyone else here?" asked Sister Germaine.

Helen looked towards the door again. The trouble was that there *was* no one else there.

"Well?" prompted Sister Germaine. "Where are you going?"

Helen fiddled with the bag of sweets in her pocket. "Oh, nowhere, Sister Germaine. We were just going for a walk." Helen had always thought that Sister Germaine would have made a wonderful grandmother. She was sweet and gentle, she was kind and uncritical, and she was usually asleep. At the moment, however, Sister Germaine was unusually awake.

"A walk?" she asked, her eyes on Helen's. "A walk where?"

Helen was usually quite good at answering direct questions with something that wasn't a lie but that wasn't exactly the truth either. At this moment, she was so surprised by Sister Germaine's manner that she said the first thing that came into her head. Which this time happened to be the truth. "We were going to walk around the barn."

"The barn?" Sister Germaine folded her hands in front of her as though she were about to pray. "Why would you want to take a walk around the barn? You girls have never shown any interest in walking around the barn before." Helen chewed slowly on her sweet, staring at Sister Germaine's hands.

"The truth, Helen," said Sister Germaine.

Helen looked up. Why hadn't she ever realized how sharp and piercing Sister Germaine's eyes were before?

"The truth?" repeated Helen.

Sister Germaine nodded. "Or I'll have you making balls of yarn for the rest of the term," she said softly. And so Helen told her the truth.

"You know," said Sister Germaine when Helen was through, "I once rode a motorcycle in Africa. The sky was pink and purple and filled with birds." She sighed. "It was very exciting." Sister Germaine put an arm around Helen's shoulder. "You know," she said, steering her towards the door, "I think I might just take that walk with you."

Sister Vincent's voice was fading in and out. "But think of what ... mean ... help..." she was saying. "But ... for the convent ... and don't forget ... and shopping..."

Helen pressed her ear to the weathered wall of the barn. To her left, Sister Germaine had her ear pressed to the wall; to her right Sara hers; on the other side of Sara, Isobel was lifting her glasses out of the dirt.

"But I..." said Sister Vincent. "My brothers ... and a Tiger 110..."

Helen frowned, concentrating. Had Sister Vincent said her brothers had a tiger? It wasn't easy to catch everything that was being said inside. Sister Vincent was speaking in a soft, cautious voice, but Mother Margaret Aloysius wasn't speaking much at all. Not unless you counted "Humph" and "Really?" and the occasional cough as speaking. Nonetheless, Helen had no trouble picturing the expression on the Reverend Mother's face as another "Humph" came through the wall. She would be peering over her glasses and her lips would be pressed so tightly together they would almost have disappeared. Her face would be talking up a storm.

"What's going on?" Helen, Isobel, Sara and Sister Germaine all turned round with a start. Sister Francis was standing behind them with a basket of dead leaves in her hand, looking surprised. She obviously hadn't expected to find them crouched together at the side of the barn like spies. Beside her was Sister Simon, covered in clay.

Sister Germaine held up her hand. "Shhh…" she hissed. "Sister Vincent is trying to convince Mother Margaret Aloysius to let her repair the motorcycle."

"What motorcycle?" asked Sister Francis.

Helen moved over as Sister Francis squeezed in between her and Sister Germaine.

"Sister Vincent's motorcycle," Helen whispered.

"What motorcycle?" asked Sister Simon.

"It's a Vincent Black Shadow," Sara explained.

"It's very old."

"Shhh…" hissed Sister Germaine.

Mother Margaret Aloysius had not only decided to speak at last, she had decided to speak loudly. Her voice came clearly through the rotting walls of the barn. "There is nothing to discuss, Sister Vincent," Mother Margaret Aloysius was saying in her dismissive way. "We have no money for this sort of nonsense… No buts, Sister Vincent…"

"But, Mo—"

"As long as you're one of us, you'll behave like one of us. Even if we did have the money, no nun of mine is going to be lying on the ground with a monkey-wrench in her hand, covered in grease." Helen put her hand over her mouth and looked at Sara. Sara, too, was trying not to laugh. Sister Germaine giggled.

Sister Vincent raised her voice, too. "But, Mother Mar—"

"No buts, Sister Vincent. There are young, impressionable girls here. What sort of example would that be setting for them?"

"A very good example, I should think," said Sister Vincent.

"Really?" asked Mother Margaret Aloysius.

It seemed to Helen that Mother Margaret Aloysius made "Really?" sound not like a question but a statement. She made it sound like "Amen". Sister Vincent didn't think so. She thought "Really?" was a question.

"Yes," said Sister Vincent. "Yes, I do. After all, Reverend Mother, surely you'd agree that part of true happiness is knowing what you're good at, doing it well and enjoying doing it. Well, one of the things I enjoy and am good at is motor mechanics." She raised her voice a little more. "And besides, Reverend Mother, the Lord did put the motorcycle here. Surely He wouldn't have done that if He hadn't intended—"

Mother Margaret Aloysius coughed. "I'm sure, Sister, that the Lord intended no such thing," she said firmly. "If the Lord had intended us to ride on motorcycles He would have given us helmets intead of habits." She coughed again.

While the Reverend Mother was busy coughing, Sister Vincent took the opportunity to complete a few more sentences. "But, Mother Margaret Aloysius," she insisted, "the Lord did give us the ability to create motor-cycles, you can't argue with that. And He did leave this one here. With my name on it. Don't you think that might be a sign? I do think He must have intended us to use it."

Mother Margaret Aloysius had stopped coughing. "No, I do not think it's a sign. If the Lord intended anyone to ride that contraption, it was not a group of ageing nuns, it was young men in black leather with rings through their noses."

"What contraption?" whispered Sister Francis.

"Sister Vincent's motorcycle, of course," Sister Simon whispered back.

Sister Germaine gave them both a cross look. "Shhh!"

Footsteps moved across the barn. Helen had never before heard footsteps sound so annoyed. "No motorcycle," said Mother Margaret Aloysius. "We're nuns, not pop stars."

"But, Mother Margaret Aloysius!" called Sister Vincent. She was almost shouting. "I do think—"

"Well, don't!" thundered the Reverend Mother. "I'll do the thinking round here. I always have and I always will!" The barn door opened with an angry groan. Mother Margaret Aloysius sailed out, her skirts flapping.

Six heads peered cautiously round the side of the barn, watching her go.

"I knew she wouldn't like it," said Helen.

"I knew it, too," said Sara.

"Now we can't make thousands of pounds and save the school," said Isobel.

"Now there's an idea..." said Sister Germaine.

"Wouldn't like what?" asked Sister Francis.

Something creaked above Helen and a chip of wood hit her on the head. She looked up. Sister Vincent was hanging out of a window at the top of the barn, watching them.

"Wouldn't like our motorcycle," said Sister Vincent. She turned her face to the sky and smiled. "The one I'm going to fix," she added. She was still smiling. It almost seemed to Helen that the sun was smiling back.

MOTHER MARGARET'S ASTHMA STARTS ACTING UP

Sister Vincent was spreading her tools out on one side of the table. Sara stood next to her, her head to one side as though she was trying to work something out. "I thought you were giving me a hand with this," said Sister Vincent.

Sara came out of her reverie. "I don't understand how you got it from the barn to the basement," she said. "Wasn't it very heavy?"

Sister Vincent passed her a set of spanners. She really must try to steer Sara's curiosity into some useful channel. "I'm stronger than I look," said Sister Vincent.

Sara took the spanners, but she was still staring at the engine. "But even so," she argued, "without a cart and a winch and pulley…"

"Helen!" Sister Vincent turned her attention to the entrance of the laundry room, where Helen and Isobel were wrestling with a portable blackboard. "If you would put that chocolate bar away, you'd have two free hands."

"But I need it for energy," grumbled Helen, stuffing the half-eaten sweet into her pocket.

Sister Vincent pointed to the left of the work table. "Over here. Where I can reach it easily."

Helen started dragging the board across the room, pulling Isobel with it.

"Lift!" ordered Sister Vincent. "Don't make so much noise. You know the Reverend Mother's asthma's been acting up again."

"Do you think it's because we're disobeying?" asked Isobel as she and Helen finally came to a stop beside the table, dropping the blackboard with a thud.

The dark eyebrows arched over the pink frames of Sister Vincent's glasses. *Patience*, Sister Vincent warned herself. *Remember you are meant to be learning patience.*

"Isobel Macauley," she said very patiently. "How many times do I have to tell you? We are not disobeying."

Isobel blinked behind her own clear frames. "But Mother Margaret Aloysius said you couldn't fix the motorcycle..."

Caution and curiosity, thought Sister Vincent. *What a combination.* Sometimes she couldn't decide who was more annoying, Isobel with her worrying or Sara with her nosiness, but at the moment it was definitely Isobel. "The Reverend Mother never said I couldn't repair the motorcycle, Isobel," Sister Vincent informed her, struggling not to sound just a little impatient. "What she actually said was that there was no money for repairing the bike."

"But—" bleated Isobel.

"And in any event, I am not repairing it." She laid a line of wrenches beside the spanners. "I am simply doing my job." She gave Isobel a patient look. "And that, in case you've forgotten, is to teach motor mechanics." She put a dented acetylene torch behind the wrenches. "If you'll all please take your seats, that is what I'll do. Teach motor mechanics."

"But are you sure Mother Margaret Aloysius doesn't think that we're disobeying?" asked Isobel as she sat down on one of the three chairs positioned in front of the blackboard.

"Izzy!" Helen gave her a nudge. "Mother Margaret Aloysius doesn't know, does she? That's why we're in the basement."

"Helen!" Sister Vincent rapped on the table. "Less talk and more attention, please." She picked up a piece of chalk. "First we will go through the basic tools. Then I'll give you an overview of the engine. Then we'll take the engine apart." She smiled, patiently. "Now, are there any questions before we begin?"

One hand shot into the air. In a class of twenty or thirty, Sister Vincent might have ignored that hand, but it was impossible not to notice it in a class of three. "Sara?" said Sister Vincent.

"I still can't work out how you got it down here," said Sara.

Mother Margaret Aloysius's head nodded sleepily over the book she was reading. It was a very long book on the Roman Empire. Mother Margaret Aloysius was practising for her retirement, when she would finally have the opportunity to read all the long books on empires and wars that she'd been meaning to read for the past forty years.

Her eyes closed. She saw a Roman soldier walking awkwardly into the study. Instead of a shield he carried a motorcycle tyre. Instead of a pike he carried an enormous spanner. He hit the tyre against the doorframe and dropped the spanner with a clang. The Reverend Mother's eyes flew open and she sat up, listening. Surely that sound had been real. She turned to the window behind her, but even in the fading light she could see that the courtyard was empty and the barn doors were closed and bolted.

Mother Margaret Aloysius frowned. Ever since Sister Vincent showed her the motorcycle, she'd been hearing odd sounds – and having odd dreams. Sister Francis was giving her an infusion of balm for her hearing, but it hadn't helped. She still heard things she shouldn't be hearing. Or didn't hear things she should be hearing – like now. Mother Margaret Aloysius strained her ears. The house was silent. Too silent for a weekday evening. Why wasn't Sister Francis banging around in the kitchen? Why weren't the girls playing their music? Why wasn't Sister Simon whirring away at her wheel? Where was Sister Germaine?

The Reverend Mother began to cough. By now Sister Germaine should have brought her pre-supper cup of wood betony tea, Sister Francis's cure for chest complaints. Is this a test? wondered Margaret Aloysius, her eyes falling on the crucifix on the wall. Was that why the asthma was coming back? Was that why she was hearing things? Was that why she'd been lumbered with Sister Vincent? But tested for what? Surely she'd proved her sincerity and dedication by now. Surely the Lord couldn't be upset with her because she'd decided to retire?

Mother Margaret Aloysius looked down at the book on her desk. She began to cough. Perhaps the Lord was as tired of the Romans as she was. She coughed again.

"Sister Germaine!" she called. "Sister Germaine!" There was no answering sound of footsteps hurrying down the corridor. "I'll just have to get my tea myself," the Reverend Mother decided. She shut the book and got up from her desk and was just about to step outside the study when all the lights went out. From somewhere in the distance she heard a faint but heartfelt scream.

While Sister Vincent was beginning her first class in motor mechanics, and Mother Margaret Aloysius was thinking about Roman soldiers carrying spanners, Sister Francis was climbing into the loft.

"A little to the left," Sister Francis directed. Her voice was muffled because her head was through a trap door in the ceiling and she had a screwdriver between her teeth. "Higher."

Sister Simon grunted. "My arm's getting tired."

"It won't be much longer," said Sister Francis. Strands of wire hung over her shoulders and clung to her skirt. She removed the screwdriver from her mouth. "I've got the blue wire in the centre whateveritis," she announced. "Now what, Sister Germaine?"

Sister Germaine was standing at the foot of the ladder, holding a small torch over a book. She squinted at the diagram. "Now you put that other wire in the thingummy on the left. Or is it the right?

Sister Francis glanced down at her. "Left or right, Sister Germaine? We'll all be blown to kingdom come if we get the wires crossed."

The torchlight wavered. "I can't stand like this much longer," said Sister Simon. "And I do have something in the kiln, you know."

Sister Francis mumbled a quick prayer for strength. "Bring the book here, Sister Germaine," she said when her prayer was done. "Let me take a look."

Sister Germaine looked up. There was nothing to see beyond Sister Francis but darkness. "I'm not really very good on ladders..." She took a step backwards rather than forwards. "I have no head for heights."

"Pretend you're picking apples," ordered Sister Francis.

"Please," begged Sister Simon. "I really don't think I can do this much longer."

Sister Germaine didn't budge. "But I don't pick apples."

"Well, pretend you do," snapped Sister Francis.

Her rosary clicking nervously, Sister Germaine climbed the worn wooden rungs behind Sister Francis. "Left, right," she muttered to herself. "Right, left."

"Hurry!" called Sister Simon.

"Closer," ordered Sister Francis. "You're still too far away."

The ladder trembled. Sister Germaine's

voice trembled. "I really don't think…"

"There! That's fine." Sister Francis bent down to read the book, bobbing before her like a cork on the sea. "May St Athanasius pray for us," said Sister Germaine.

The torch light bobbed. "Is he the patron saint of electricians?" asked Sister Simon.

"No," gasped Sister Germaine as the ladder shook again. "He died when a piece of masonry fell on his head."

"Got it!" cried Sister Francis, disappearing back into the hole.

"What in the name of the holy apostles is going on here?" demanded a new voice. The voice of Mother Margaret Aloysius. For just a few seconds, the three nuns were frozen in the light of the Reverend Mother's torch: Sister Simon standing on top of a sheep the size of a footstool; Sister Germaine three quarters of the way up an extension ladder, holding on to the wall with one hand and Sister Francis's skirt with the other, looking like a large beetle on a small piece of straw; Sister Francis halfway into the ceiling, the Giant going up the beanstalk. And then the beanstalk broke. Everyone screamed, but none screamed louder than Mother Margaret Aloysius.

"But you can't make an omelette without breaking some eggs, can you?" asked Sister Vincent.

The heating system rumbled.

Sister Vincent sighed. "It is unfortunate that what broke this time was the Reverend Mother's temper," she admitted. "But at least the Sisters were taking some initiative. That's what matters."

A radiator clanked.

Sister Vincent slowly chewed on a slice of onion. "After all, if we're going to change things around here, then something has to happen. I should think that would be apparent to anyone, don't You?" The clock ticked, the curtain rustled in the draught.

After the lights went out, and Isobel screamed, and Helen dropped half a packet of malted balls on the floor, and Sara had been prevented from investigating, the four of them had sat by the beam of Sister Vincent's torch, quietly discussing the fuel pump and its function while they waited for the power to come back on. The power didn't come back on. Instead, there was a rather horrific series of crashes upstairs.

"You lot wait here," she'd ordered the girls. "Don't move till I call you. That means you, too, Sara." To be on the safe side, she'd taken the torch and gone to see what was wrong. After everyone had been set back on their feet and Sister Francis had explained what had happened, Sister Vincent tried to calm Mother Margaret Aloysius. "There really isn't anything to be upset about, Reverend Mother. You can't make an omelette without breaking a few eggs, can you?" It was then that Sister Vincent had been asked to go to her room.

Even though Sister Vincent had had nothing to do with the attempt to repair the electrics, the Reverend Mother was still angry with her. "I have no idea what you're on about, Sister Vincent," she'd gasped. "But I do know that I would feel a lot less like a broken egg myself if I didn't see you for a while. Perhaps I'll feel stronger in the morning."

Obediently, Sister Vincent had taken a cup of tea and a cheese sandwich and gone to her room, where she was now, talking things over with the Lord.

"The Reverend Mother is a very difficult woman to help," said Sister Vincent. "You'd have thought she would at least have thanked me for turning the electricity back on." She sipped her tea. "And for helping her and Sisters Germaine and Simon up. And for getting Sister Francis down from the ceiling." The clock ticked on, a light rain began to fall. "But, no," said Sister Vincent. "She blamed me."

Mother Margaret Aloysius wasn't even a little grateful. Instead, she held Sister Vincent responsible for everything that had happened. "It's you, isn't it?" she'd kept saying over and over. "It's all because of you." It was just as well that Mother Margaret Aloysius hadn't decided to find out what her youngest nun had been doing in the basement. Although Sister Vincent knew that she wasn't really disobeying the Reverend Mother's orders, she wasn't sure that the Reverend Mother, discovering the Black Shadow engine in pieces on the laundry sorting table, would entirely agree. Sister Vincent put her cup down on the bedside table. "I suppose she wouldn't have been so upset if Sister Germaine hadn't been blue," she continued. "Or if Sister Simon hadn't been standing on that sheep. Or if Sister Francis hadn't been swinging from the trap door with a screwdriver between her teeth."

She removed another slice of onion from her sandwich. "Still," she said, "I don't know what that has to do with me. I didn't tell Sister Francis to have a go at repairing the electrics. I didn't tell Sister Germaine to dye miles of wool. I didn't suggest that Sister Simon start making giant sheep." She bit into the onion. "Did I?" she asked, her eyes on the ceiling.

Despite Sister Francis's mending of the wiring, the bedside lamp flickered.

"Only technically," said Sister Vincent. She chewed slowly. "It does make you wonder who Mother Margaret Aloysius blamed for everything before I got here, though, doesn't it?" she asked. This time, the clock continued ticking and the rain continued falling but the lights didn't flinch. "You're right, of course," said Sister Vincent. "She didn't need to blame anyone. Nothing ever happened before I got here." Sister Vincent lay back with a contented smile. "I must be on the right path, then," she said. She closed her eyes and listened to the comforting sound of the rain. If things at St Agnes kept changing at this rate, the convent wouldn't be recognizable soon. Assuming Sister Francis didn't blow it up, of course. "I think this could turn out to be quite some omelette," she said.

Helen's stomach growled with hunger. Not only was supper late, but Sister Vincent had confiscated her supply of chocolates during the class on motor mechanics and hadn't given them back. To get her mind off her stomach, she rubbed more soap on her hands. Helen had been in the bathroom trying to scrub the dirt from her inspection of a carburettor off her hands ever since Sister Vincent sneaked them back upstairs. Sister Vincent had rushed them past the kitchen, where the other nuns were, like mice scurrying by a sleeping cat.

"We don't want to upset the Reverend Mother any more than she has been by having her worry about what you were all doing in the basement," she'd explained. "I'll give you a shout when supper's ready."

But that had been hours ago, and there had been no shout to come down to supper, so Sara and Isobel had gone to check. They wouldn't let Helen come because her hands would give them away. Helen hadn't minded. She'd started composing her next letter to her father in her head. She imagined him laughing over the story of Sister Francis falling out of the loft. Helen sighed. She was beginning to mind now, however. Isobel and Sara had been gone for ages. She rinsed her hands again. Her fingers were wrinkled, but still black.

"Don't tell me you're still at it," said Isobel, suddenly charging into the room.

"That's one of the many advantages of dark skin," said Sara, right on her heels. "Dirt doesn't stand out in the same way."

Helen looked up. Her stomach emitted another growl, but she made an effort, and put the question of the welfare of the Sisters before the question of the whereabouts of her meal. "Are they all right?" she asked.

"Sister Germaine's blue," said Isobel, "but that's because of the dye, not the fall. And Sister Simon landed on a bag of wool, so she's all right, too, though the sheep she was standing on broke."

"Sister Vincent got the ladder to Sister Francis in time, so she's all right," said Sara, sitting on the edge of the tub.

"She says it's lucky she did gymnastics as a girl."

"What dye?" asked Helen.

Isobel slid onto the laundry hamper. "The dye Sister Germaine's been using on her wool. Apparently she's decided to make wall hangings instead of scarves. She's trying to capture the colours of Africa in wool."

"And Sister Simon's making sheep instead of saints," said Sara.

Helen put down the nail-brush. It seemed impossible. Sister Germaine had been knitting beige scarves and Sister Simon had been making statues of obscure saints for as long as she could remember. Why would they change now?

"Why?" asked Helen.

"For the same reason Sister Francis decided to fix the electrics," answered Isobel. "Sister Vincent."

Sara was nodding. "Because of what Sister Vincent said about doing what you're good at and what you enjoy."

Helen made a face. "I bet Mother Margaret Aloysius isn't too pleased."

"Not too pleased," said Sara. "She sent Sister Vincent to her room."

"But she's coughing too much now to really shout," added Isobel.

Helen's stomach growled again. "What about supper?" she asked.

Isobel looked at Sara. Sara looked at Isobel.

"I knew we'd forgotten something," said Sara.

SISTER VINCENT IS REMINDED OF PERU

Patience, Sister Vincent told herself as thunder rumbled outside. This is only a minor setback. She checked off the name Al's A-1 Auto Repairs on her list. That's all, a minor setback. After all, the rocker box wasn't built in a day.

Still reassuring herself, she stepped over a cracked headlamp socket, out of the dark, dank garage and into the afternoon.

Rain poured down. The grey stone buildings of Little Anstis huddled together beneath a sky like bilberry jam, and the inhabitants of Little Anstis huddled beneath their anoraks and umbrellas. Behind the town, the neat fields and woods seemed almost to have melted away. Sister Vincent pulled up her hood. Al, proprietor of Al's A-1 Auto Repairs, waved goodbye from beneath a Volvo, but Sister Vincent was occupied with her own thoughts and didn't see.

"Peru," said Sister Vincent as she soggily pedalled away on Isobel's old bicycle. "That's what this reminds me of – Peru." A red estate wagon sped past, splashing her with muddy water.

"No, not the rain," said Sister Vincent as she started up the road. "Not that it doesn't rain in Peru. It rains quite a bit, actually. No, I was thinking of the time the tent fell on me. On that mountain. Remember?" Another wave of muddy water broke over Sister Vincent as a Cherokee Jeep whizzed by.

The problem of saving the abandoned children in Peru had been a difficult one, but she hadn't realized quite how difficult until the tent collapsed.

As usual, she had started out full of enthusiasm and resolution, only to be stopped short by something she hadn't planned for. She'd been barrelling along, thinking she was going the right way in the right direction – thinking she had everything under control – only to discover suddenly that she wasn't and she didn't. She'd been going the wrong way, in the wrong way, all the time. She had nothing under control. In Peru, it had been the collapse of the tent that pulled her up short. Until that moment, she'd thought she knew what she was doing. But when the tent suddenly caved in on her in the middle of the night and she'd found herself being hurried into the back of a truck, she'd understood that she didn't. She didn't have a clue. "And that's exactly how I'm feeling now," Sister Vincent confided as she headed back to St Agnes. "That I've left something out." A white sedan raced around her, horn honking.

"No, I really don't think my not being patient enough has anything to do with it," said Sister Vincent. "I admit that I may have overlooked a few details, just like I did in Peru. But I really do feel that the problem is too much enthusiasm, not too little patience." Al's had been the last garage on Sister Vincent's list. There were only three auto-repair shops in the area. M & S – Your Local Reliable Garage, Frank's Friendly Motors and Al's A-1. She'd been hoping that at least one of them might have some old bike parts lying around that she could use, and that they would let her have for nothing. But not one of them had. M & S and Frank had all said the same thing as Al. "Sorry, Sister, but I'm afraid you're out of luck. You're not going to find what you need around here. Maybe in the city…"

She leaned forward, breathing heavily as the push-bike climbed a hill. In Peru, Sister Vincent had overlooked the determination of her enemies. This time what she'd overlooked was the impossibility of actually fixing the motorcycle. "Those are mistakes anyone could make." Sister Vincent panted as she marched into a gust of wind, still striving for patience. She'd been so optimistic when she found the bike, but the fact was that the Black Shadow must have been sitting in the barn for nearly forty years. How had she thought she was going to repair it? If she had a workshop she could make most of what she needed herself. If she could get to the city she could buy the parts she couldn't make. But she didn't have a workshop. And even if she could get to the city, she didn't have any money. Then, too, even if she had the right tools and the right parts, she still had a problem. She couldn't work on the Black Shadow in the basement because Mother Margaret Aloysius would be bound to hear her. She couldn't work on it in the barn because there weren't any lights.

"Not that I'm discouraged, Lord," said Sister Vincent as she coasted down the hill. "I wasn't discouraged in Peru and I'm not discouraged now. I just need a little time to rethink the situation." A van went by like a moving fountain. "Of course, in Peru I had that long drive through the mountains, wrapped up like a sausage in a roll in the back of the truck, to reconsider the situation," said Sister Vincent as she reached the lane that led to St Agnes. "Here I have Mother Margaret Aloysius watching me all the time. She's waiting for me to do something else wrong. There's no time to sort things out properly."

Sister Simon and Sara were at the foot of the lane, positioning a large ceramic sheep on either side of the gate. One of the sheep was blue and had a torch in its mouth; the other was black and wore glasses. They waved. Sister Vincent didn't wave back. She was still talking to the Lord.

"The only time the Reverend Mother isn't watching me is when she's busy or asleep," she was saying as she reached the front of the house. She sighed. "It really would be helpful if she would go away for a few days. Perhaps somewhere dry." She glanced up as the trees shook. Sister Germaine and Isobel were at the living-room window, putting up a large hanging of a herd of oryx running across the desert. They waved.

Sister Vincent didn't wave back. "I was thinking of the Reverend Mother," Sister Vincent remarked as she rode on towards the back of the convent. "A little holiday might help her asthma."

Sister Francis and Helen were dragging a heavy cable through the basement window and across the courtyard, partially hiding it in the border shrubs. Sister Vincent pulled up beside them. "What are you doing?" she asked.

"Running electricity into the barn," said Sister Francis. Sister Vincent glanced at the house.

Helen blew a large blue bubble. "Mother Margaret Aloysius is taking a nap," she said.

As it happened, however, Mother Margaret Aloysius was not taking a nap. She'd tried to take a nap, but she couldn't stop worrying about Sister Vincent and the effect she was having on the other Sisters long enough to fall asleep: Sister Francis turning into a handyman... Sister Germaine abandoning the knitting of scarves... Sister Simon making gigantic sheep... She'd tossed and turned and coughed, and then just lay listening to the rain. It was the only sound to be heard. Where was everyone? Why was no one ever where she was supposed to be when she was supposed to be there?

And that is why, as it happened, Mother Margaret Aloysius wasn't resting, as everyone thought, but standing in the doorway of the living-room. The look on her face suggested that although she was in a familiar place, something had happened to make it strange. That there were bears skating over the carpet or a lake where the sofa should have been, for instance. In fact, there were no bears and no lake in the living-room.

But there was some kind of rug hanging in front of the window. Galloping across the rug was a group of antelope. Hanging over them was what the Reverend Mother assumed must be the sun, although it was not the colour of the sun that usually shone over St Agnes. It was a purplish red. A purplish red sun in a pink and orange sky. Smiling up at the rug as though it had every right to be where the curtains once hung were Sister Germaine and Isobel.

Mother Margaret Aloysius wheezed. "What in heaven's name is that?"

Sister Germaine and Isobel stopped smiling. They both looked round.

"Oryx," said Sister Germaine. She grabbed the stepladder and started busily folding it up.

"Oryx?" Mother Margaret Aloysius looked from Sister Germaine to Isobel. "And what, precisely, are these oryx doing on our living-room window?" she asked.

Isobel glanced at Sister Germaine, but she was busy fiddling with the catch on the ladder. "They're cutting down on the draught," said Isobel quickly.

Mother Margaret Aloysius folded her arms in front of her. "Is that right?"

"Sister Vincent suggested it," said Sister Germaine. "She was worried about your chest."

"Oh, was she?"

Sister Germaine opened her mouth to answer, but before she could speak Sister Simon and Sara burst into the room. They were soaking wet and laughing.

"That's the lot!" boomed Sister Simon.

Mother Margaret Aloysius turned around. "The lot of what?"

Sister Simon and Sara stopped laughing and stood there dripping on the carpet.

Sister Simon recovered first. "W-w-why, Mother Margaret Aloysius," she stammered. "I thought you were taking a nap..."

"Well, I'm not taking a nap," snapped the Reverend Mother. "I'm waiting for an answer to my question. The lot of what?"

"Sheep," said Sister Simon, concentrating on unzipping her anorak. "Sister Vincent said you wanted them out of the house."

Mother Margaret Aloysius wheezed again. "What I said was that I wanted them out of my sight."

"And they are out of your sight," broke in Sara. "They're in the meadow and down the lane and—"

"Sister Vincent!" Mother Margaret Aloysius flapped past Sister Simon and Sara and into the hall. She'd been too lax, that was where she'd gone wrong. It was the asthma. The asthma had weakened her, distracted her. "Sister Vincent!" The Reverend Mother huffed and puffed towards the kitchen. "Sister Vincent!" The kitchen was empty. "Sister Vincent!"

Mother Margaret Aloysius wrenched open the back door and stepped into the rain. Sister Vincent, Sister Francis and Helen were all kneeling at the side of the courtyard, doing something to the shrubs.

"Sister Vincent! Sister Vincent, just what do you think you're doing?"

Sister Vincent turned slowly around. "Would you believe that we were praying?" she asked.

"No," said Mother Margaret Aloysius, striding forward. "No, I would not." In her preoccupation with the figures kneeling in the shrubbery, the Reverend Mother failed to see the cable stretched across the yard. Her foot caught and she shot forward, landing with a cry of pain in the bushes beside Sister Vincent.

"Most of us use our rosary beads for prayer, Sister Vincent," said Mother Margaret Aloysius with as much dignity as she could summon under the circumstances. "Not extension leads."

DISCOURAGEMENT FALLS UPON SISTER VINCENT LIKE A COLLAPSED TENT

Sister Francis came into the room sideways, the newly-repaired television in her arms.

"This is very good of you, Sister," Mother Margaret Aloysius was saying. Because she'd twisted her ankle when she tripped in the courtyard, Sister Francis was making her stay in bed. "Very good indeed." She shifted the poultice on her swollen foot.

"Ugh," said Sister Francis as she and the television set lurched towards the bureau.

"I'm sure that there isn't much on that I'll want to watch," Mother Margaret Aloysius commented. "But there's always the news, of course. And documentaries. I've always been rather fond of those."

"Umph," said Sister Francis. She dabbed at her forehead with the hem of her veil. She knew it was uncharitable, but she was beginning to wonder if fixing the television had been as good an idea as she'd originally thought. What she'd imagined was herself, the other nuns and Helen, Sara and Isobel watching films together in the living-room and eating popcorn, not the Reverend Mother watching wildlife documentaries and complaining about having to stay in bed. But the Reverend Mother had been laid up for only a few hours and already she was beginning to get restless.

Mother Margaret Aloysius began flipping through the TV listings. "Who was that at the door?" she asked.

Sister Francis dabbed at her forehead again. No, she decided, it was far better to miss a few films than to have Mother Margaret Aloysius bored and looking for something to do. At least the television would keep her occupied.

"Door?" repeated Sister Francis. Perhaps she shouldn't have fixed the front bell after all.

"Yes, door." The paper rustled. "I distinctly heard the doorbell and Sister Germaine talking to someone in the hallway for quite some time."

"Oh, that." Sister Francis plugged in the set. "Just some visitors."

"Visitors?" The paper rustled again. "What kind of visitors?"

"Just visitors," answered Sister Francis vaguely. She removed the plug, examining it closely for bits of dust. She could feel the Reverend Mother glaring at her back.

"What are you talking about, 'just visitors'? We never have visitors at St Agnes, just or otherwise. No one ever stops here unless they're lost or they're selling something."

"Well, they do now," Sister Francis said to herself. She blew at the plug. Which was the reason it was important to keep Mother Margaret Aloysius occupied, and upstairs. It wouldn't help her asthma to realize just how many visitors the convent was attracting lately.

Satisfied with the cleanliness of the plug, Sister Francis turned on the set. "It was only someone curious about the convent," she said out loud.

"Curious about St Agnes?" The bed springs creaked as the Reverend Mother sat up. "What's there to be curious about?"

A field full of ceramic sheep, for one thing, thought Sister Francis. But of course the Reverend Mother hadn't been downstairs in days, and so she hadn't seen Sister Simon's sheep grazing in the meadow, or Sister Germaine's knitted scenes of Africa hanging from every window in the house. But others had. People who hadn't realized the convent existed before were stopping by to ask about the sheep, and staying to admire Sister Germaine's handiwork and drink Sister Francis's teas. Sister Francis became engrossed in the tuning knobs. "It is a very old building," she murmured.

"Old building?" echoed the Reverend Mother. "What does that have to do with anything? It's always been an old building and no one's ever been interested in it before."

Sister Francis stepped back with a flourish. "How's that? The colour all right?"

Distracted, Mother Margaret Aloysius stared at the set. "May the Apostles pray for us!" she murmured, trying to take in what she was seeing. She leaned forward, peering over the top of her glasses. "What in heaven's name are those people doing, Sister Francis?"

"Bungie jumping," said Sister Francis.

Sister Francis stood at the sink, happily filling bottles with a brownish liquid that smelled rather like billy-goats. Since the advent of the visitors, quite a few people had become interested in her remedies and teas. It was giving her new scope for experimentation. In fact, the advent of the visitors was giving all the nuns new scope for experimentation. Sister Germaine had started knitting scenic windsocks as well as her hangings, and at that very moment, Sister Simon was sitting at the table, wrapping a very large duck with bead-yellow eyes in black scarves. Major Irving, who had a farm on the other side of the valley, had seen the sheep at the foot of the lane and asked her to make him a duck. She was thinking she might branch out into chickens or even goats. They both looked up as Sister Germaine entered the room.

"How is she?" Sister Francis asked over her shoulder.

"She's watching that series on the Amazon," said Sister Germaine. "I must say, she's becoming very concerned about the future of the morpho butterfly."

Something clanged loudly outside. Sister Francis glanced nervously towards the ceiling. "I prefer it when she watches the game shows. They make so much more noise, she never hears the front bell or Sister Vincent working on the bike."

"I'm just glad that the Reverend Mother's relaxing a bit," said Sister Simon. "She's so involved in her programmes that she forgets to worry about us and what we're doing without her to tell us what to do." She carefully lifted the duck into a cardboard box. "Did you know she's even started watching the music programmes?"

"Pop music?" Sister Germaine put the tray containing the remains of the Reverend Mother's supper on the counter. "But Mother Margaret Aloysius loathes pop music."

"I think she's getting used to it." Sister Simon tore off a strip of sellotape. "She does seem to know quite a bit about the drums."

"She told me she wanted to be a jazz drummer when she was a girl," said Sister Francis.

"Fancy that. After all these years, she only just told me. She used to practise on her mother's pots and pans."

Sister Germaine slowly scraped the dishes into the bin. "You know, I think Mother Margaret Aloysius is actually having a good time," she said. "It's been ages since she's shown so much interest in the outside world. She even asked me what tortilla chips and roller blades were." There was another, louder clang beyond the courtyard. Sister Francis peered out of the window to where a dull light glowed through the cracks in the walls of the barn. "I'm glad someone's having a good time," she said.

"Poor Sister Vincent..." Sister Simon sighed. "It's such a shame that she can't get that bike of hers going. She seems to have so much hope pinned on it."

Sister Germaine sat down at the table. "I know what you mean." She took up the knitting she'd left there earlier and went back to the windsock she was making of a family of hippopotamuses bathing in a pool. "You'd almost think she believes it would solve all our problems."

Sister Francis wiped her hands on her apron. "That's ridiculous, of course," she said. Her eyes went to the window again. "But it does still seem a shame that the rest of us are enjoying our... our hobbies and Sister Vincent isn't."

"There must be some way we could help her," suggested Sister Germaine. She squinted critically at a hippopotamus ear. "Perhaps if we—" She broke off as the back door opened and Sarah, Helen and Isobel trooped in with a gust of rain. Sara was carrying a motorcycle repair manual, Helen was chewing on a stick of liquorice, and Isobel was wiping oil from her glasses.

"How's it going?" asked Sister Francis. "Any improvement?"

Helen shook her head. "Not really. Every time she sorts out one little thing she discovers something she can't sort out."

"She has to rebuild the engine," said Isobel glumly, sitting down beside Sister Germaine.

"Mains, rebore and pistons," said Sara.

Helen wiped liquorice from her mouth. "Plus we have to regrind the valves."

"And we need new tyres," said Sara.

Sister Francis was staring at the pot of green liquid. Maybe Sister Germaine is right, she was thinking. Maybe there is some way we could help Sister Vincent. She stirred her decoction thoughtfully. "I suppose what she needs are some spare parts she could make do with," she said almost to herself.

"Exactly what I was thinking," said Sister Germaine. She gazed musingly at her hippopotamuses. "And I suppose a workshop where Sister Vincent could do all this grinding and boring would help," she added.

Sister Simon looked up from sealing the box closed. "And money," she said, frowning at the roll of sellotape in her hand. "A little money would come in handy."

Isobel, Sara and Helen sighed. "Sister Vincent says we'll need a miracle," said Sara.

Sister Francis put on the kettle. "What's needed here," said Sister Francis, "is some nice strong woodruff tea."

Sister Vincent was sitting on the floor of the garage, a spanner on her lap, leaning against the motorcycle and talking to the Lord.

"I don't usually ask for much help," Sister Vincent was saying, "but I could do with a little now." Rain poured in from the broken roof. "This is not impatience," she said, glancing above her. "This is realism." Sister Vincent fidgeted a cylinder head between her hands. "As You know, Lord, I could repair this bike, but it is a little difficult when I can't get the parts." The cylinder head fell through her fingers and rolled under a rusted paraffin stove. Sister Vincent picked up the spanner.

"And even if I could improvise," she went on, "what would I do about the things I can't make myself?" She started thumping the spanner against the ground. Rain splashed into the puddle on the floor of the garage. Sister Vincent shook her head. "You see," she said, "I was right. It is just like Peru. I thought I knew what was happening, I thought it all made sense, and now I realize that it doesn't and I don't. I'm right back where I started." She threw the spanner to one side. "Worse. When I started I had hopes. Now all I have is a tent wrapped around me." The spanner bounced back and hit her on the foot.

"Yes," said Sister Vincent. "Yes, I do feel discouraged."

She sighed like the woman without hope that she was, but resisted the urge to give the spanner a kick. "I know I shouldn't feel discouraged, but it's not only that I have a tent wrapped round me," she continued. "The tent's wet, Lord. It's wet and I'm beginning to feel as though there are quite a few insects and lizards in here with me." It was true, the tent was enveloping her. She couldn't see or hear or find the exit. Sister Vincent's resistance crumbled. She kicked the spanner.

Although she hadn't kicked it all that hard, the spanner slid effortlessly across the ground. She watched it vanish under a broken bookcase. Sister Vincent looked around for something else to bang, but most of the things that had been near her were already scattered around the barn. "And even if I do fix the bike, what difference would it make?" she demanded. "It isn't going to make Mother Margaret Aloysius change her mind, is it? It isn't going to save the convent. Not even a Vincent Black Shadow could do that." All that could be heard was the plopping of raindrops. Sister Vincent raised her eyes to the roof. "I know You must have a plan, Lord," said Sister Vincent, "but I do wish You'd let me know what it is."

The rain stopped suddenly, as though someone had turned off a tap. Something creaked behind her. Sister Vincent looked warily round as the garage door slowly swung back. A dark figure holding an umbrella in one hand and a tray in the other stood in the entrance.

"I thought you might like a little snack," said Sister Francis, bustling over to the circle of light where Sister Vincent sat. "There's nothing like a cup of tea and a nice honey flapjack when you're feeling a little low."

"That's very kind of you, but I really—" Sister Vincent began.

"I thought it might be nice for your guest," whispered Sister Francis, setting the tray down on the stack of papers beside her.

"Guest?"

Sister Francis looked over at the doorway. "Major Irving!" she called. "Major Irving, don't stand out there in all that rain. Do come in!"

Sister Vincent looked around as a second dark figure loomed in the doorway. It was the fat man from the bus. The man with the duck.

"Well, Sister, I see you found your convent all right."

Sister Vincent was rarely speechless, but at the moment she could only nod and glance at the roof again. A single star glimmered through the hole.

"Funniest thing," Major Irving boomed. "All these years, I never knew you ladies were up here and then one day I'm driving past and I see these sheep, and I think to myself, I wonder if I could get the artist to make me a tufted duck. I love tufted ducks. And when I realized this was a convent, well, I told the other Sisters about meeting you..." He laughed. "What a coincidence, wouldn't you say?"

Sister Vincent had the strangest sensation that she was being unwound from a wet tent. "Coincidence," she mumbled, continuing to nod.

Major Irving's eyes went past her and stopped on the dismantled motorcycle. "That's the bike Sister Francis was telling me about?"

Sister Vincent looked around, but Sister Francis had slipped from the barn. She nodded again. "Yes, it's—"

"A Vincent!" Major Irving stepped over an exhaust pipe and went closer for a better look. He clapped his hands together. "Great bikes. Real character. I rode to Madrid on a Vincent in 1955. Not a Black Shadow, I'm afraid. It was an old Rapide. Went with a chap named Edkins. Met him in the war."

"Oh," said Sister Vincent, her head bobbing up and down. Remembering the day on the bus, she slipped her hands into the pockets of her jacket.

The Major turned to her. "But you don't want to hear about me and Edkins any more than you want to hear about ducks." He winked. "I understand that you're looking for a workshop."

She really wished that she could stop nodding. "Yes," said Sister Vincent. Her fingers touched something. "I need to—"

"Cobble together some parts, Sister Francis said. Just like the war. We all had to learn to make do." He laughed. "You should have told me when we met on the bus. Could have saved yourself a bit of time." He started patting his jacket. "You ring me in the morning, Sister. I think I have just what you need." He patted some more. "I'll give you my card if I can find one."

Sister Vincent removed her hand from her pocket. In it was a small rectangle of heavy paper. She held it up. "I already have one," said Sister Vincent. She could feel discouragement rise from her shoulders like a collapsed tent being raised.

THE REVEREND MOTHER DOESN'T GIVE A BUTTON FOR DENMARK

Sister Germaine froze in the doorway with her armful of clean linen. The Reverend Mother's bed was empty. The stacks of books and magazines meant to help keep her busy sat on the bedside table, untouched. The television was off. Mother Margaret Aloysius was standing at the window, staring into the courtyard. Sensing trouble, Sister Germaine began to back out noiselessly.

Mother Margaret Aloysius turned around. "There you are," she said, sounding as though Sister Germaine had been hiding from her. "If you don't mind, Sister, I'd like you to tell me precisely what is going on."

Sister Germaine halted, holding the linen against her like a shield. "On?"

"Yes, on." Mother Margaret frowned. "You may dress like a penguin, Sister Germaine, but you sound more and more like a parrot every day. Why do you repeat everything I ask you?"

Sister Germaine stepped into the room. "Do I?" she asked.

"Yes," said Mother Margaret Aloysius. "You do."

Sister Germaine put the linen down with a sigh. Now that the Mother Superior's ankle was better and she could move around more, it was getting harder and harder to keep certain things a secret from her. "I wasn't aware—" began Sister Germaine.

"Well, now you are," snapped the Reverend Mother. She scrutinized Sister Germaine over the rims of her glasses. "What's going on? Precisely. It's bad enough that there always seems to be some stranger tramping around the garden, but the lot of you are up to something, and I have a right to know what it is."

Sister Germaine dropped the sheets on the chest of drawers as though they'd suddenly become hot. "I'm afraid that I'm a little busy at the moment, Mother Margaret Aloysius," she said, starting to edge backwards again. "I'm helping Sister Francis with—"

The Reverend Mother's voice rolled over hers. "Firstly, I would like to know what those things you have flapping all over the courtyard are."

Sister Germaine blinked, wondering what the best answer might be. The trouble was that she enjoyed knitting windsocks so much that once they were done it seemed unkind not to hang them in the wind. She forced a smile on her face. At least Mother Margaret Aloysius hadn't realized that they were flapping all over the front lawn and down the lane as well.

"Windsocks."

"Windsocks." The Reverend Mother gazed at her impassively. "And Sister Simon and the girls? What do they think they're doing to the barn?"

"Painting a mural." It wasn't the whole truth, but it was enough to be getting on with.

The whole truth was that the Sisters had hoped, wrongly it seemed, that the sight of the mural being painted might at least distract Mother Margaret Aloysius from noticing the ever-increasing number of visitors to the convent.

Mother Margaret Aloysius fingered her rosary. "Painting a mural. I see."

Sister Germaine avoided meeting the eyes of the crucifix over the bed. "Sister Simon thought it would cheer the place up a bit," she explained.

"How thoughtful of her." The Reverend Mother's smile locked. "And what are you all doing, sneaking things out of the barn? Is that to cheer the place up, too?" Sister Germaine could feel her own smile set. Apparently the painting of the mural hadn't distracted the

Reverend Mother from noticing that either.

"We're clearing out the barn." This, of course, was not the whole truth, either. Mother Margaret Aloysius looked thoughtful. "Clearing out the barn? After all these years?"

The whole truth was that they were clearing out the barn so that Sister Vincent could set up her workshop. Major Irving was giving her the tools and equipment she needed to rebuild the motorcycle, as well as some spare parts and a small forge, all of it left behind by the previous owner of Gunga Din. She nodded.

"Sister Vincent felt it would give the girls something to do. You know how restless they get."

Mother Margaret Aloysius continued to look thoughtful. "At night? I distinctly saw Sister Vincent and the girls carrying things out of the barn last night. There's something fishy going on, don't tell me there isn't."

Sister Germaine flinched under the Reverend Mother's steel-blue stare. " 'There's something rotten in the state of Denmark'," she murmured under her breath.

Mother Margaret Aloysius' stare became steelier. "What are you babbling about now?"

"It's from *Hamlet*," explained Sister Germaine. " 'There's something rotten in the state of Denmark'."

"Denmark?" snapped Mother Margaret Aloysius. "I don't give a button for Denmark.

It's St Agnes I'm worried about."

The narrow road that wound through the woods was badly paved and unlit, and empty except for an old truck with the words GUNGA DIN DUCK FARM painted on the side. The truck was moving very slowly. Hunched over the wheel was Sister Vincent. Beside her, squeezed together on the rest of the seat, were Sara, Helen and Isobel. It was raining. If it hadn't been raining it would merely have been the sort of black and shapeless night the country-side is particularly good at, but the rain made it seem as though they were driving through the sea. All four were peering through the windscreen as though trying to spot mosquitoes.

"We're lost, aren't we?" said Helen.

For the first time since she arrived at St Agnes, Sister Vincent wished that Helen had a mouthful of chocolate.

"Of course we're not lost," said Sara confidently. "Sister Vincent knows exactly where we are."

"Watch out!" screamed Isobel as something suddenly loomed directly in front of them.

Sister Vincent slammed on the brakes. It was a tree. "Good glory," she said, straightening out her wimple. "What's that doing there?"

Something heavy and metal crashed to the

floor of the back of the truck.

Helen pressed her face to the side window. "I think we've left the road," she announced.

Sister Vincent closed her eyes. "Patience," she reminded herself. "You have got to practise patience."

"Helen's right," said Sara, her nose against the windscreen. "We're in the woods."

"I knew this would happen," said Isobel. "Now we're going to be stuck here all night and Mother Margaret Aloysius is going to find out we're gone, and then we'll never get the bike fixed and the school will close, and I'll be sent to some orphanage in France—"

Practising patience, Sister Vincent closed her eyes and counted to ten. Perhaps it had been a mistake to bring the girls with her after all. Originally, the Major himself was going to deliver the equipment, but he'd strained something getting the forge into the truck and was laid up in bed. She'd thought the girls would enjoy the adventure, but Isobel wasn't really cut out for adventure. Isobel worried about every little thing.

Helen opened the door and leaned into the rain. "I think I see the road," she said. "At least there's something that doesn't have anything growing on it."

Sara handed her the torch. "Here," she said. "See if this helps."

Helen leaned out further; rain blew in. "I see

a stone wall," called Helen. "I don't remember seeing a stone wall on the way over."

"Neither do I," said Sara.

"We didn't pass one," said Isobel.

Sister Vincent snapped on the overhead light and took the map from the dashboard. She stared at it. "I don't understand it," she mumbled. "I normally have a very good sense of direction." She'd never even got lost in L.A. That's the countryside for you, she told herself. No lights, no signposts, and everything looks the same in the dark.

Sara leaned over. "Where are we meant to be?"

Sister Vincent pointed to two thin, black parallel lines, weaving through a patch of green. "I turned left at the fork, so we should be somewhere around here."

"I don't see any stone wall," said Sara.

Sister Vincent sighed. "No," she said. "Neither do I."

Helen shut the door. "Izzy's good at geography," said Helen.

Sister Vincent looked at Isobel, squashed between Helen and Sara, still worrying about being sent to France. "Izzy?"

Isobel took the map. She squinted at it through her glasses. She raised her head and squinted through the windscreen. She turned back to the map. "We're there," said Isobel.

Sister Vincent, Helen and Sara all stared at

the point where Isobel's fingernail touched the map.

"We can't be there," said Sister Vincent. "That's miles out of our way."

"There's the stone wall," said Isobel. "And there's that little bridge we came over."

Sister Vincent frowned. Little bridge? What little bridge? "Oh, of course, the little bridge."

"And see?" Isobel pointed again. "There's that double curve."

Little bridge, double curve... If Isobel weren't sitting beside her, Sister Vincent would almost have thought they'd taken different routes. "You *are* good at geography, aren't you?"

Isobel nodded. "I want to be a cartographer. I want to make Ordnance Survey maps."

Sister Vincent put the truck in reverse. "Helen," she ordered, "look out of the back again and make sure we don't hit anything. Sara, wipe off the windscreen." She glanced at Isobel. "And you," she said, "will navigate."

Once they were back on the right road, Sister Vincent taught them all a song about pirates.

"There they are!" cried Sister Francis in a low voice. "I see lights at the bottom of the lane."

Sister Germaine jumped. She was so nervous that she put her left arm in the right-hand sleeve of her anorak. "This isn't going to work," she whispered. "Mother Margaret suspects something, I'm sure she does."

Sister Francis pulled on her coat. "Do stop fussing, Sister Germaine," she ordered. She took her torch from the table and put it in her pocket. "Whatever Mother Margaret suspects, it can't possibly be the truth."

Sister Germaine considered this for a second. Sister Francis had a point, of course. The Reverend Mother would never guess in a million years that her nuns were setting up a motor repair shop in the barn under cover of darkness. On the other hand, Sister Germaine wasn't really worried about what the Reverend Mother was thinking, she was worried about getting caught. In the thirty-odd years she'd been at St Agnes, Sister Germaine had never done anything that the Reverend Mother didn't approve of – until Sister Vincent arrived. Since Sister Vincent arrived, all of them seemed to have got quite accomplished at doing things the Reverend Mother wouldn't approve of. And now here she was, sneaking out in the middle of the night like some sort of bandit.

"But what if she hears us?" she insisted. "What if—"

"Hears us?" Sister Simon pulled up the hood of her raincoat. "Sister Vincent's taken care of everything." She raised her eyes towards the ceiling. "Listen."

Sister Germaine listened. Although she hadn't seen the record player since 1964, the year Mother Margaret Aloysius declared war on pop music, she could hear an album playing over their heads. It seemed to be in the middle of a drum solo.

"What in heaven's name is that?"

"Shelly Manne," said Sister Simon as they started to follow Sister Francis down the hall towards the back door. "I don't know how Sister Vincent knew, but he was Mother Margaret Aloysius' favourite."

Anyone watching from the house would have seen the three elderly nuns of St Agnes, their coat collars pulled up and their heads bent low, scurry through the rain like spies and disappear into the barn.

Anyone watching from the house would have seen the Gunga Din Duck Farm truck, its lights dimmed, round the side of the house, and heard four female voices singing, "Let the sky be our roof and the stars our chandeliers and the wind for ever at our backs..." as the truck coasted into the courtyard.

And anyone watching from the house would have seen the barn doors open, the truck vanish inside, the barn doors close – and the night settle down again as though nothing had happened.

But there was no one watching from the house.

Mother Margaret Aloysius was sitting in her chair beside the record player, her eyes closed. She was listening to the music, but she was also thinking and remembering. She was thinking about all the dreams and plans they'd once had for the school, and how exciting St Agnes used to be. She was trying to remember when she'd given up fighting and made the other Sisters give up fighting too. She was thinking about the windsocks flapping in the trees and the sheep dotted around the field and the mural Sister Simon and the girls had painted on the barn. And she was trying to remember the last time anyone had acted without her permission.

"Denmark, indeed..." Mother Margaret Aloysius muttered to herself.

But her fingers were tapping on the arm of the chair, her foot was tapping out the beat on the floor. She smiled to herself as she remembered the sight of Sister Francis hanging from the ceiling and Sister Germaine and Sister Simon in a heap on the floor. Maybe they all weren't as old and tired as she'd thought. She smiled again. Denmark, indeed...

WHO CAN HELP SISTER VINCENT IN AN ABNORMAL WORLD?

"And what, may I ask, are these?"

Sister Germaine stopped in the doorway of the Reverend Mother's study as though suddenly turned into a pillar of salt, or perhaps concrete. She'd left the study only long enough to answer the door, thinking the Reverend Mother was up in her room, listening to one of the records Sister Vincent had lent her. Which she wasn't. Instead, the Reverend Mother was sitting stiffly at her desk, holding in her hands the papers Sister Germaine had been going through when she was called away. The way she held them, they might have been a gun.

Sister Germaine finally recovered her voice. "Mother Margaret Aloysius!" she cried. "What in heaven's name are you doing out of your room? Sister Francis said it would take at least two more days before you could really walk on that ankle again."

"Don't start acting solicitous, Sister Germaine," interrupted Mother Margaret Aloysius. "My foot's good enough for hobbling around a little." She eyed the deputy head sternly. "What I want, Sister Germaine, is not solicitude but an explanation."

"An explanation?" whispered Sister Germaine.

"Yes, an explanation." Mother Margaret Aloysius shook the papers in her hand. "Exactly what are these?" she demanded. Sister Germaine quietly shut the door behind her and stepped into the room. She had been so busy worrying about the Reverend Mother finding out about the workshop in the barn that it hadn't occurred to her to worry about the Reverend Mother discovering the applications she'd left on her desk.

"Well ... um..." Sister Germaine dithered, fumbling with the glasses that hung around her neck.

Mother Margaret Aloysius leaned forward. "I really don't see how you could have forgotten what they are so quickly," she said. "You haven't been gone for more than fifteen minutes. But perhaps you'd like me to refresh your memory." She shook the papers again. "They're applications, Sister Germaine. Applications for St Agnes's school."

Sister Germaine stared back, too surprised

to speak. As unlikely as it seemed, the Reverend Mother must have been watching her all the time; following her around to see what she was up to. An image of the Reverend Mother hiding in the hallway, waiting for Sister Germaine to leave the room, came into her head. In this image, the Reverend Mother was crouched behind the aspidistra in a very undignified, un-Reverend Mother sort of way. Mother Margaret Aloysius was glaring. It was difficult to tell whether she was angry or simply astonished.

"Who in the name of the saints in heaven is applying to St Agnes?" she wanted to know. "Can you answer me that, Sister Germaine? Who?"

Sister Germaine cleared her throat. "Quite a few people, actually…" she began.

"I can see that." Mother Margaret Aloysius dropped the forms on the desk and folded her hands in front of her. "What I should like to know is how and why."

Sister Germaine wished she could look at something other than the Reverend Mother's piercing blue eyes, but they held her as firmly as a vice. She tried again to explain.

"Well, as you know, Mother Margaret, we have had all these visitors lately … and I guess they're intrigued … curious…"

Mother Margaret Aloysius said nothing, but continued to stare at her. Which had an effect on Sister Germaine rather like an injection of truth serum.

"You know," babbled Sister Germaine, "intrigued with Sister Francis's little pharmacy … and Sister Simon's sculptures … and my knitwork…Curious about Sister Vincent's class—" She came to an abrupt stop in the middle of the word "classes".

"Sister Vincent's classes?" Mother Margaret Aloysius repeated. "But Sister Vincent doesn't teach any classes."

Sister Germaine's lips moved up and down. "Helps," she bleated at last. "Sister Vincent helps me with my classes."

"Does she now?"

Sister Germaine nodded eagerly. "Yes… Yes, she does. And she's very good too, Reverend Mother. The girls love her. She's very stimulating."

"So is a cold shower," answered Mother Margaret Aloysius, "but it's a lot less trouble." She leaned back, looking thoughtful. The thin lips got thinner; the blue eyes narrowed. "Are you trying to tell me that all these visitors are so taken by what they see of St Agnes that they want their children to go to school here, Sister Germaine? Is that what you're trying to tell me?"

Sister Germaine nodded again. "That's right, Mother Margaret Aloysius. They—"

"Are being led up the garden path," the

Reverend Mother finished for her.

Sister Germaine blinked. "Pardon?"

"Don't act innocent with me," snapped Mother Margaret Aloysius. "You know there are no places at St Agnes." She tapped the papers with her fingertips. "Why are you accepting applications for St Agnes's school when St Agnes's school will be closing at the end of the term, Sister Germaine? Can you tell me that?"

Sister Germaine considered this question for a few seconds, wondering if there was some way of answering that wouldn't infuriate the Reverend Mother even more. "Well," she said at last, "Sister Vincent felt—"

"Sister Vincent," echoed the Reverend Mother. "Of course. Sister Vincent had to have a hand in this. And I suppose that Sister Vincent also felt that you should not only accept applications, but you should encourage them as well."

Again, Sister Germaine considered the question. "Excuse me?"

The thin lips almost vanished; the blue eyes became slits. "Don't deny it, Sister Germaine. I heard you with that couple at the door. You were giving them a sales pitch." Sister Germaine gaped. The Reverend Mother really had been following her around. Not only had she been crouched behind the aspidistra outside the study door, she'd been crouched behind the coatstand at the foot of the stairs.

"I don't believe this," said Sister Germaine. "You've been spying on me."

Mother Margaret Aloysius gave her a look. "When in Rome do as the Romans do," she answered. "Or should I say, When in Denmark do as the Danes?"

Helen was sitting at her desk, writing another letter to her father. This time she was telling him how they'd got lost in the Gunga Din duck truck and how Isobel had guided them home. She was sure her father would find it funny, especially the part where Sister Vincent hit the tree.

Helen smiled to herself. Gone were the days when all she had to write about were what weed they'd had for dinner or how Sister Germaine had fallen asleep in the middle of something again. Now they didn't eat weeds, and Sister Germaine never fell asleep in the middle of anything. Helen smiled again. Her father really seemed to be enjoying her letters. Not only was he writing back, he'd sent her the tool kit he'd had when he was a teenager. "This is what I used on my first motorbike," he'd written. Helen hadn't known her father had ever had a motorbike.

Helen glanced over at her companions. Isobel was staring unseeingly out of the window, thinking probably. Isobel had been thinking a lot since the night she navigated them safely home. Sara was sitting at her desk, reading through a manual Sister Vincent had lent her on rebuilding carburettors. Sister Vincent said that Sara showed real promise as a mechanic. "It's because you always want to know how things work," Sister Vincent had decided. "What's nosey when it comes to people is useful when it comes to cars."

"Listen," Isobel ordered suddenly. Helen had gone back to finishing her description of Sister Vincent yelling, "Good glory, how did that get in the middle of the road?" and didn't look up. Nor did Sara.

"Helen!" Isobel shouted. "Sara!" Helen threw down her pen with a scowl. Besides thinking a lot lately, Isobel had become much bossier.

"What is it, Izzy?" snapped Helen. "Can't you see I'm doing something?"

"And me," put in Sara. "I'm busy, too."

Isobel held up her hand. "Listen," she repeated. She gestured towards the walls and ceiling. "What do you hear?" Helen shoved her letter aside and made a show of listening. Music throbbed down the hallway from the Reverend Mother's room. Above them, Sister Francis whistled along as she repaired something in the loft. Below them, Sister Germaine and Sister Simon were laughing in the kitchen.

Helen shrugged. "What?" she asked. "I

don't hear anything."

"It just sounds normal to me," agreed Sara. A saxophone started to play and Sister Francis changed her tune.

"But you do hear something," Isobel insisted. She raised her eyes to the overhead light. "Don't you see? It didn't use to sound like this. Normal was when it was so quiet all the time."

More than the quiet, Helen remembered when she used to wonder if it were possible to die of dullness. "It wasn't completely quiet," she said. Dullness didn't seem any more normal than quiet now. "You could hear the roof leaking and things falling off the building."

Sara cocked her head. "Izzy's right. The convent does sound different…" She listened, concentrating. "I think it sounds more alive."

Helen looked down at her letter, imagining her father smiling as he read it. "And happier," she added. "It sounds much happier, too."

"And it's all since Sister Vincent came," said Isobel. "It's all because of her."

"It's true," said Sara. "She's changed things at St Agnes."

Sister Vincent, thought Helen, her eyes on Isobel but her mind on Sister Vincent. Sister Vincent's the one person who doesn't seem any happier. Even though Sister Vincent had been able to rebuild a lot of the motorcycle thanks to Major Irving's workshop, there were still some things – things like tyres – that had to be bought, and her disappointment was beginning to show. While everyone else's spirits were rising, Sister Vincent's were lowering. She spent most of her time shut in the barn, banging away and talking to herself.

"It doesn't seem fair that she's worked so hard and she still can't get the Black Shadow on the road, does it?" Helen said at last. "Even if we can't save the school and we all have to leave at the end of the year, it would be nice if Sister Vincent could at least have that."

Sara picked up the plastic model of an internal combustion engine that Sister Vincent had given her from her desk and started to fiddle with it. "But there isn't anything we can do about it, is there?" she asked.

"I've been thinking," said Isobel, looking thoughtful. "Maybe there is something we can do about it. Maybe if we all chipped in – you and me and Sister Germaine and Sister Francis and Sister Simon – maybe we could get Sister Vincent what she needs for the bike." Her voice became excited. "You know, surprise her with it as a present." A fresh wave of laughter rolled up from the kitchen. The Reverend Mother put on a piano boogie and Sister Francis stopped whistling and began to sing along.

Helen gazed at Isobel in open admiration. It

was such a good idea, she couldn't imagine why she hadn't thought of it. "I wonder..." she murmured.

A smile of understanding came over Sara's face. "You mean as a thank you."

"Exactly," said Isobel. "As a thank you."

Helen, however, started shaking her head. "It won't work," she decided. "Even if we have enough money, we don't know what she needs, except for tyres."

"There's a list," said Isobel. "I saw it yesterday when I brought her her tea."

"Izzy's right," said Sara. "There is a list."

Isobel beamed at her. "And you're just the person to get it," she said.

Sara, idly poking at the things on Sister Vincent's workbench, knocked two wrenches and a notebook to the floor.

"Sara!" Sister Vincent turned off the blowtorch and pushed the goggles back on her head. As if she weren't having enough trouble, Sara had decided to spend the afternoon haunting her. "What's got into you today? That's the fourth time you've done that. Isn't there something you could be doing in the house? Why don't you see if you can't burn supper or break some of Sister Simon's sheep?"

"I'm sorry." Sara bent down to retrieve what she'd dropped, scooping up the feeler gauge, the notebook and the papers that had fallen out of its pages. "I didn't mean to—"

"I'm not interested in what you meant to do," said Sister Vincent sharply. "I'm interested in what you are doing." She snatched the things from Sara's hands and put them back where they'd been. "And what you are doing is getting in my way."

Normally, she might have wondered why the neat and orderly Sara was suddenly so messy and clumsy, but as far as Sister Vincent was concerned, nothing was normal anymore. Everything was abnormal. L.A. had been normal. London had been normal. Peru had been normal. After the tent had collapsed on her in Peru, she'd realized what she'd been doing wrong and she'd got onto the right path, moving in the right direction. The way she always did. But that hadn't happened this time. She'd got out of the tent, thanks to Major Irving, but she needn't have bothered. She might as well have stayed where she was. Because she wasn't going in the right direction, she still seemed to be going in circles.

Despite her best efforts, the Black Shadow was never going to be roadworthy, and even if it were, it seemed less and less likely that it would make a difference to anyone. "But, Sister Vincent," said Sara, "I only wanted to help." Once again, she knocked against the workbench and everything crashed to the floor.

This time, Sister Vincent didn't even bother to look round. "I'm not sure you can help me, Sara," she said. She glanced towards the roof, but she didn't seem to be getting much help from on high at the moment either.

Mother Margaret Aloysius wiggled her right foot, which was still in a bandage and had started to ache, while she crouched beside the kitchen door. The Reverend Mother was becoming accustomed to crouching in hallways, even with a bad ankle. She had no choice. She was a practical woman and it had become apparent to her that crouching in hallways was the only way she would ever learn what was going on, so she crouched.

Through crouching she had learned that there were parents waiting to enroll their children in the school. Through crouching she had realized that Sister Germaine, Sister Francis and Sister Simon had a lot more fight and spirit in them than she'd thought. Through crouching she had come to understand that Helen, Isobel and Sara considered the convent their home. Through crouching she had discovered what was going on in the barn. And at the moment crouching was teaching her just how much everyone cared about Sister Vincent. Mother Margaret Aloysius wiggled her foot again and put her ear against the door. Crouching had also taught her that she herself had a lot more fight and spirit left than she'd thought, too – but that she'd been too stubborn to see what had to be done.

"We need two hundred and fifty-six pounds and forty-nine pence," said Sister Germaine. She put down her pencil and looked round the table. "Approximately."

Sister Francis smiled encouragingly. "Well, that's not exactly a fortune these days, is it?" she asked brightly.

"The Prime Minister probably spends more on lunch," said Sister Simon.

Isobel, who had been carefully counting the money they'd all chipped in, looked up. "It's two hundred pounds and fifteen pence more than we have," she announced. The others turned to her.

"Two hundred?" asked Sister Germaine.

"And fifteen pence," said Isobel.

Helen bit the head off a jelly snake. "Are you sure?" she asked. "Did you count in my sweet allowance for the rest of the month? There's a couple of extra quid—"

"I counted it in," said Isobel. "And my pocket money, and Sara's pocket money, and what's left from the money Sara's parents sent her for her birthday."

Sister Francis snatched the paper away from Sister Germaine. Her lips moved as she ran her finger up and down the columns of figures. "Two hundred and fifty-six pounds and forty-nine pence," she said at last. She looked round the table. "Where in the name of heaven are we going to get that much money?" she asked.

Sister Simon shrugged.

Sister Germaine sighed.

Helen bit the head off another jelly snake.

Sara twiddled the bead on one of her plaits.

Isobel shook her head.

Mother Margaret Aloysius got slowly to her feet. There was another thing crouching in hallways had shown Mother Margaret Aloysius, and that was that, as Sister Vincent had tried to tell her, there was more than one way to tune an engine. She opened the door and strode into the kitchen. Six heads turned to look at her.

"Mother Margaret Aloysius!" cried Sister Germaine. "What are you doing—"

The Reverend Mother folded her hands in front of her. "I've been listening outside the door, that's what I've been doing," she said, her eyes darting from one guilty face to the next.

Sister Francis cleared her throat and met the Reverend Mother's eyes. "How long?" she asked.

The blue eyes shone like ice. "Long enough."

Sister Germaine got to her feet. "I can explain, Mother Margaret ... if you'll just give me a chance."

"I'll do no such thing, Sister Germaine."
Mother Margaret Aloysius crossed the kitchen
and sat down in the chair beside Helen.

Sister Simon began to protest. "But surely,
Mother—"

Mother Margaret Aloysius thumped her
fist on the table. "We don't have any time to
waste with your excuses," she said. A slow
smile spread across her face. "I'm going to tell
you how we'll get that money."

ST AGNES HELPS THE LORD

It was a grey, wet and windy day in Little Anstis. Sister Germaine and Helen came warily out of the stationer's carrying two large cardboard boxes wrapped in plastic and tied with string.

Sister Germaine poked her head out of the doorway. "I do hope the bus isn't too late," she mumbled, gazing into the deserted street. "I don't fancy waiting in the rain for too long."

Helen's stomach rumbled. She'd been having quite a good time this morning. First there was the bus ride. Helen had shown Sister Germaine some of the photographs her father had taken in Africa, and Sister Germaine had told her about each place. Some of her stories had been so funny that the whole bus was laughing by the time they reached town. Then there was the excitement of rushing around in the rain, buying supplies. Suddenly, however, Helen realized how hungry she was. They'd had to leave the convent before breakfast in order to catch the first bus, and that had been hours ago.

"I don't suppose we have any change left for a cup of tea," Helen suggested, without any hope that there was. On the few occasions when she'd accompanied one of the Sisters shopping there had never been any change left for a cup of tea.

Sister Germaine began to fumble in her pockets. "Well, let's see, shall we? We did buy all that plastic thread for the chimes and the windsocks ... and we took every scrap of tissue paper in the stationery shop, including the stock for Halloween and May Day..." She pulled out a few silver coins with a triumphant cry. "But I do believe we have enough left for a pot of Earl Grey and even a cake." She lifted her black umbrella in front of them like a shield and started down the high street. Helen loped beside her.

"You didn't think Sister Vincent looked suspicious?" asked Sister Germaine as she skirted around another large puddle. "I'm not really sure she believed us."

"Sister Vincent always looks suspicious," answered Helen, who was rather enjoying the puddles. "It's because she's lived in places like Los Angeles and London." She landed beside

Sister Germaine with a satisfying splash. "And, anyway, I'm sure she believed you. She knows you always tell the truth."

"But that's just the point," Sister Germaine continued with a sigh. "I don't always tell the truth anymore. In all my years, I never told a lie to anyone. Until now." She sighed again. "Now I seem to be telling them all the time."

Helen shook her head. "It wasn't really a lie," said Helen with authority. Not only had she had more practice with fibs than Sister Germaine, but watching the way Sister Vincent handled the telling of the truth had given her an extra bit of confidence in the matter. "All you did was tell Sister Vincent that we couldn't help her this morning because we were going to the hospital to visit the sick. It was for her own good, so it's a fib, not a lie."

Sister Germaine peered down at Helen through her rain-spattered glasses. "I'm not so sure the Lord would agree with you on that."

Helen, however, was sure. "But how else could we get out of the convent without Sister Vincent?" she reasoned. "You know how restless she's been lately. If she knew we were coming to town she would have wanted to come along. And then we wouldn't have got our shopping done. And then we wouldn't be ready for the fair next weekend." She dodged as the wind blew an empty carrier bag their way. "And then we wouldn't have the money to finish fixing the Black Shadow to surprise her."

"Well, when you put it like that…" Sister Germaine came to a stop in front of the Blue Cup Café. She put her hand on the knob and opened the door. Helen, right behind her, found herself with her face in the back of Sister Germaine's raincoat. "What's wrong?" asked Helen.

Sister Germaine put her hand out, as if holding Helen back. "It's Sister Vincent!" she whispered. "She's here!"

Cautiously, Helen peered around the side of Sister Germaine. There, indeed, was Sister Vincent, sitting in the corner with a cup of tea and a motorcycle manual. "How did she get here?" asked Helen. "She wasn't on the bus with us and the next one's not due for twenty minutes."

"Never mind that." Sister Germaine turned and started pushing Helen through the door. "We have to get out of here. I certainly don't want to have to lie to her again."

Helen glanced over at the window of the café as Sister Germaine dragged her past. Out of the corner of her eye, she could see Sister Vincent gazing out at them, a puzzled expression on her face.

"It won't be a lie," said Helen, turning her attention to the ground ahead of them. "It'll still be a fib." Nonetheless, the image of Sister

Vincent's eyes on them still clear in her mind, she was relieved that she wasn't the one who would have to make it up.

Isobel followed Sister Simon from the bus. "I hope Sister Vincent isn't waiting for us when we get back," Isobel was saying as she stepped into the rain. "I don't think she believed that we both had headaches."

"I feel badly about avoiding Sister Vincent so much, too, but what else can we do?" Sister Simon set her tartan trolley on the pavement with a sigh. "We'd never get ready in time for the county show with her hanging around."

Isobel pulled up the hood on her anorak. "It's just that I think she's taking it personally," said Isobel. "You know, that her feelings are hurt." Yesterday, Sister Vincent had asked Isobel if she wanted to learn how to rebore a piston. Isobel, who had no interest in or talent for reboring anything, knew that Sister Vincent had asked her out of desperation because both Sara and Helen were doing something else.

"Oh, no, I don't think so."

Sister Simon opened her umbrella and gave it a shake. "St Agnes is a working convent, after all. I'm sure Sister Vincent understands how busy we all are."

"But we didn't use to be so busy," Isobel pointed out.

"No, but we are now," said Sister Simon. "As it is, I'd never get all my sheep painted in time without your help. You really are very good at detail work, you know."

Isobel was so pleased by the compliment, that she instantly forgot her concern about Sister Vincent. "What shall we do first, then?" she wanted to know. "Shall we pick up the new cards?" Sister Simon and Isobel had designed the card together. There was a drawing of the convent at the top and the name, address and telephone number below it.

Sister Simon pointed the umbrella at the building in front of them. "As we're already here, I think we should nip into the chemist's for the Reverend Mother's toothpaste first." She started pulling the trolley. "And then on to the art supply shop for the cards and the paints."

Isobel shot forward to get the door for Sister Simon but it opened before she could touch it.

"Sister Vincent!" Isobel gasped. "What are you doing here?"

Sister Vincent looked from the figure closing the umbrella to Isobel. "I might ask you the same thing," she said coolly. "I thought you were ill." Isobel took a step backwards onto Sister Simon's foot.

"Headache tablets," answered Sister Simon, shoving Isobel forward again. "We'd run out, so Isobel and I thought we'd just pop into town and get some."

"You two must be planning on quite a few headaches," said Sister Vincent, her eyes now on the trolley Sister Simon was squeezing past her. "I see you've come prepared to get a good supply."

Two people walked slowly along the unpaved path leading through the field to the convent. The taller of the two held a large black umbrella and the shorter pulled a garden wagon with high wooden sides. The two were Sara and Sister Francis. They'd been out since just after breakfast, going from door to door collecting old bottles to put Sister Francis's remedies in. "There's still two more farms to visit," Sister Francis was saying as the wagon clinked along. She looked at her watch. "We'd better try and go a little faster. If Sister Vincent comes back from her walk and I'm not still repairing the washing machine and you're not still doing your homework, she'll wonder why we said we were too busy to go with her."

"I knew we should've come up with better excuses." Sara grunted. The wagon wasn't easy to pull in good weather on a solid road, but the rain and the mud were making it very difficult to keep it moving.

"There wasn't time," said Sister Francis, jumping neatly over a puddle. "She caught me off guard. And we couldn't very well go with her, could we? We had to get these extra bottles today if we're going to be ready for the fair."

Sara ploughed on. "I just hope we make enough money to buy the things Sister Vincent needs."

"And I hope Mother Margaret Aloysius has a chance to examine the bike while Sister Vincent's out of the way, so that we buy the right parts."

Sara, however, was still worrying about Sister Vincent. "It's just that she seems to be getting sadder," said Sara. "I'm always hearing her in the garage, talking to the Black Shadow."

"Oh, I wouldn't worry about that," said Sister Francis dismissively. "You know Sister Vincent, she's always talking to something. I once found her deep in conversation with a holly bush."

Sara was about to say that she didn't really find that reassuring when she felt herself come to a sudden stop with a clatter. "Uh oh," said Sara instead.

Sister Francis stopped, too. "What is it?" she asked, glancing over.

"We're stuck." Sara looked behind her. Only the tops of the wagon's wheels were poking out of the mud. "Very stuck," she added glumly.

"I'll get behind and push," said Sister Francis.

She shut the umbrella and put it on top of the bottles. "On the count of three, you pull and I'll push," she continued, hitching up her skirt and getting into position.

Sara kept her eyes on the top of Sister Francis's head as she leaned against the wagon.

"One…"

Something yellow flashed above Sister Francis.

"Two…"

Sara's eyes moved upwards.

"Three!" shouted Sister Francis.

Sara, however, had stopped listening.

"Three!" Sister Francis screamed again. "Three!"

"You heard Sister Francis," said Sister Vincent. "Three!" At the sound of Sister Vincent's voice, Sister Francis looked over her shoulder and Sara pulled.

"You must have both finished sooner than you'd thought," Sister Vincent commented as she helped them out of the mud.

The convent was silent when Sister Vincent returned by herself. "Sister Germaine?" she called from the hallway. "Sister Simon?" They must still be in town. "Mother Margaret Aloysius? Is anybody home?"

The old clock ticked in the stillness. Mother Margaret Aloysius was probably taking her afternoon nap. Sister Vincent looked around the dark corridor, suddenly feeling very alone.

"I haven't had a very good day," she told the empty house as she hung up her anorak. "What with Sister Germaine and Helen bolting from the café when they saw me. And Sister Simon and Isobel turning up in town after they'd said they were unwell. And Sister Francis and Sara trekking all over the countryside when they told me they had to stay in..." One of the pipes screeched.

"You're right," said Sister Vincent. "A cup of tea might cheer me up." While she waited for the water to boil, Sister Vincent talked to the ceiling lamp in the kitchen.

"I don't seem to have done too good a job here, have I?" she told the lamp. "The only thing I've succeeded in doing is getting everyone together." She smiled sourly. "Which, if anything, I've done too well." Isobel had been right about Sister Vincent. She was taking their avoidance of her personally. She'd felt very hurt this morning when everyone had some reason for not spending the day with her, but she'd been even more hurt when she realized that they hadn't been reasons, they'd been excuses. It wasn't that they couldn't spend the day with her, it was that they didn't want to. "Sister Germaine and Helen are always together," Sister Vincent informed the ceiling. "Sister Francis and Sara are always together, and Sister Simon and Isobel are always together, too."

The kettle began to whistle; Sister Vincent sighed. "But what about me? What am I meant to have learned from this?" Sister Vincent poured the steaming water into her cup. "The worst thing is that I was really beginning to like it here," she continued. "I admit that it's not as exotic as Peru, or as exciting as London, and the food isn't anything like the food in L.A., but I was starting to feel quite at – quite comfortable."

She gazed out of the window while the tea brewed, thinking of that first morning, when the girls showed her round St Agnes. A small smile crept over Sister Vincent's lips as she pictured the three of them standing in the courtyard with her, Sara asking questions, Isobel wiping her glasses on her clothes, and Helen chewing something. "It was right over there," said Sister Vincent. "I liked them immediately."

The light dimmed.

She glanced up. "Well, I could see that they had potential," Sister Vincent amended. "And I do like them now." She remembered how the three girls used to follow her everywhere. "And they used to like me," she added with a sigh. Maybe it was her fault, maybe she hadn't been patient enough after all. Maybe that was the lesson she was meant to learn at St Agnes.

Sister Vincent's stare went back to the courtyard, but instead of Sara, Isobel and Helen, what she saw was Mother Margaret Aloysius. Mother Margaret Aloysius was striding towards the house through the rain under Helen's red and white umbrella. Her lips were moving, so she must be singing. "Where has she been?" asked Sister Vincent, her eyes going to the barn. She glanced at the ceiling. "She wasn't in the barn, was she?"

The thing Sister Vincent really dreaded was that Mother Margaret Aloysius would find out that she'd been working on the Black Shadow and make her get rid of it. In all the hours she'd spent with it, Sister Vincent had become fond of the old bike. Even if it never rode again, she liked to imagine that she had the old motorcycle running again. She pictured herself riding down one of the back country roads on a clear, sunny day. Sometimes one of the other nuns was behind her, her wimple blowing out from under her helmet, and sometimes one of the girls was with her, holding on tight. Other times, though, she was on her own, just riding into the wind.

The Reverend Mother drew closer to the house and Sister Vincent faced the kitchen door. The best defence, as she'd learned in Lima, was a good offence. She wasn't going to wait to be attacked about the bike, she would attack first.

"Mother Margaret Aloysius!" cried Sister Vincent. "What are you doing out in the rain? I thought you were having a nap."

If the Reverend Mother was surprised to see her she didn't show it. She closed the umbrella and gave it a shake. "And I thought you were having a walk," she replied.

SISTER VINCENT
GETS LEFT BEHIND

Sister Vincent quietly shut the door to her room. Unable to sleep, she'd decided to get up early and work on the bike. "There's no point in giving in to depression," she mumbled as she tiptoed down the hall. "The best thing is to do something useful." Footsteps sounded over her head; a door banged shut at the back of the house. Sister Vincent stopped by the stairs to listen. Yes, she definitely heard voices – voices and something heavy being dragged across the kitchen floor. Someone laughed. "What time is it?" asked Sister Vincent. "It must be later than I thought."

She looked at her watch. According to her watch, it was almost six. But it couldn't be. At six o'clock on a Saturday morning the only ones up and busy at St Agnes were the chickens. She held her watch to her ear. It was still going. The hall clock struck six as

Sister Francis began to sing "Bye-bye Black-bird". Sister Vincent looked towards the sound of their voices. "Now what's going on?" she asked.

All week long, the other Sisters and the girls had been even busier and more elusive than before, disappearing like shadows in the dark whenever they had any free time. When she walked into a room, all laughter and talking stopped. When she went to investigate a noise in some corner of the house, there was never anything there. Sister Vincent hadn't said anything about it, though. Sister Vincent had practised patience.

Still trying to practise patience, Sister Vincent waited for a reply. Sister Francis continued to sing. Sister Vincent stood up straight. "I suppose I'll have to see for myself," she said. She took a step forward. At that exact moment Helen and Sara came thundering down the stairs, moving so fast that they didn't see her. "Good glory!" Sister Vincent exclaimed, jumping out of their way.

"Sorry, Sister," said Helen, racing past her.

"Sorry, Sister," said Sara, disappearing after Helen in the direction of the kitchen. Sister Vincent edged around the banister and glanced warily up the stairs, but to her surprise there was no sign of Isobel.

"Where's Isobel?" she asked the empty stairway. "She may be last, but she doesn't like to be left ou—ooof!"

"Oh, my dear ... Sister Vincent..." gasped Sister Germaine. "I'm so sorry. I don't know how – I didn't see you there." She peered over the pile of windsocks she was holding, clearly torn between wanting to help Sister Vincent up and wanting to continue doing what she'd been doing when she ran into her, which was getting into the kitchen as fast as she could. Sister Vincent stared back, catching her breath. What had made her think that Sister Germaine was old and frail? She hadn't been tackled like that since L.A.

"We were sure you were – I mean, I thought you were still in bed... You've been working so hard..." Sister Germaine began to edge her way down the hall.

"And I thought you'd still be in bed," said Sister Vincent, staggering to her feet. "What's everyone doing up so early?"

Sister Germaine inched away. "Up?"

"Yes, up. You, Sister Francis, Helen and Sara..." Keeping patience in mind, Sister Vincent resisted the temptation to haul Sister Germaine back by her veil. "The only ones who still seem to be in bed are Mother Margaret Aloysius and Isobel."

Sister Germaine smiled but kept moving. "Yes ... well..."

Sister Vincent could feel patience slipping away even faster than Sister Germaine. "Well, what is everybody doing?"

Sister Germaine opened her mouth, but if she did reply it was lost in the sudden sound of a three-litre engine barrelling down the drive. Sister Vincent ran to the window. The Gunga Din Duck Farm truck flew past the house, the Reverend Mother at the wheel, Isobel beside her with a duck on her lap.

"What is going on?" demanded Sister Vincent. She turned back to Sister Germaine.

Sister Germaine was gone.

"But what county show?" asked Sister Vincent. "No one told me—"

Mother Margaret Aloysius banged the doors of the truck shut behind Sister Simon and the girls and looked over her shoulder at Sister Vincent. She certainly had a talent for appearing where and when she was wanted least. The Reverend Mother had prayed that Sister Vincent wouldn't get up until she and the others were well on their way, but it seemed that even the Lord had difficulty keeping Sister Vincent out from underfoot. They'd only managed to load the truck before she got into the courtyard by locking the back door of the house and pretending not to hear her knocking.

"I'm sure you're mistaken, Sister Vincent," said Mother Margaret Aloysius, heading towards the front of the truck. "You must have heard us talking about the county show. We attend it every year." She opened the driver's door. "Don't we, Sister Francis?"

"Oh, yes, yes," boomed Sister Francis, climbing into the cab beside Sister Germaine. "Every year."

Sister Germaine nodded. "That's right, every year."

Mother Margaret Aloysius said a silent prayer that the Lord wouldn't punish them for claiming that they always went to the county show when, in fact, they hadn't been since the Mini passed on. She put the key in the ignition. The Lord was forgiving; the truck started.

Sister Vincent leaned in at the window. "But shouldn't I come with you?" she asked. "My placement may be temporary, but I am part of the convent, too."

"Of course you are," said the Reverend Mother with her eyes on the gear shift. "But I'd much prefer you to stay behind." She revved the engine. "We need you to keep an eye on things here." The truck lurched forwards. "In case something happens."

Sister Vincent trotted alongside. "In case what happens?" she called.

The gears made a grinding sound as Mother Margaret Aloysius put the truck into second. "Anything!" she shouted back as she stepped on the gas. "In case anything happens."

* * *

Helen leaned on the back of Sister Francis's chair, wishing she'd brought some sweets with her. Somehow, in the excitement of getting ready to come this morning, she'd forgotten all about them. Helen stifled a yawn. She was already feeling bored. The drive over had been exciting because a bad-tempered bull had attacked the Gunga Din Duck Farm truck. And setting up the stall had made Helen feel oddly important. Now, however, they could only wait for the customers to come – which was something the customers weren't doing. Helen watched another crowd of people pass by, eating doughnuts and talking about what they wanted to see next, which never included the wares of St Agnes.

Mother Margaret Aloysius folded her hands on the table in front of her, careful not to disturb any of Sister Francis's bottles or Sister Simon's vases and umbrella stands. "You know what this reminds me of?" she asked. Helen swallowed another yawn. Detention. You have to sit still and do nothing then, too.

Sister Germaine hooked one last wind chime above the table. "I dread to think," she said simply. "The way you drove us through that field reminded me of the time I crossed the Kalahari on three wheels." She stepped back to check the effect. "Only there were no bulls on the Kalahari, of course. Just gemsbok."

"It reminded me of that car chase in that

film we watched the other night," said Sister Simon. "Although there weren't any bulls in that either, were there?"

"It didn't remind me of anything," said Sister Francis. "I've never driven off the road before."

"Not the ride," said Mother Margaret Aloysius. "This!" She gestured around them. There was nothing but stalls and people as far as you could see. "It reminds me of Rome," she said, smiling at a man walking by with a small pig in his arms. "The markets of Rome. How I loved market day."

Helen leaned over to Sara, who, bored as well, was straightening out the jars of elderflower water. "That was because she wasn't stuck behind a stall doing nothing," she whispered. Although the number of times the horn had been used on the journey over had left Helen's ears ringing slightly, it obviously hadn't impaired the Reverend Mother's hearing in the slightest.

"You're right, Helen," said Mother Margaret Aloysius. "You're absolutely right. What have I been thinking of? Young girls shouldn't spend market day sitting at a counter with a bunch of old ladies. You three should go off and see the sights."

Helen couldn't hide her surprise. "We should?"

"Of course you should." The Reverend

Mother flicked one of the chimes. "I want you to enjoy yourselves."

Helen looked over at Sara and Isobel. She's never wanted us to enjoy ourselves before, said her look. A lot of things had changed at St Agnes recently, but the change in Mother Margaret Aloysius was the hardest to get used to.

"You do?" asked Sara.

"Of course I do."

"But we don't have any money," Isobel blurted. "We put all our money in the kitty to buy supplies."

Without so much as a blink in the Reverend Mother's direction, Sister Francis opened the shortbread tin they were using as a cash-box. "There's a little bit left over," she said. "I'm sure we could spare enough for you girls to buy some sweets and play a game or two." Helen, Sara and Isobel all looked at the Reverend Mother.

"What an excellent idea." She smiled happily. "By the time you get back we'll have sold half our stock," she assured them.

"Half a sock, more like," whispered Helen as they walked away.

Helen chewed thoughtfully on a piece of home-made fudge as they passed the fruit pie stall for the third time. "I think we're going to have face the awful truth," she said. "They've gone."

"Don't be ridiculous," said Sara. The set of

bangles she'd won tossing ping pong balls into bowls of water jangled. "They can't have gone. Where would they go?"

Helen shrugged. "How should I know, but we've been walking in circles for at least an hour and we haven't found the stall again."

They'd found the games stalls, the food stalls and stalls selling everything from candles to friendship bracelets, but there wasn't a windchime, herbal tea, wall hanging, ceramic animal or nun in sight. "We must be in the wrong section," said Sara. "We must have lost our bearings."

Isobel shook her head. "I haven't lost my bearings. I'm sure we were right over there." She pointed to a young woman selling dried flowers. "There, between the man with the honey and the hamburger stand."

"You must be wrong," Sara insisted. "It has to be a different bee man and a different hamburger stand."

Helen peered down the aisle where video games were beeping and bleeping, hidden by groups of young boys watching the players. "Maybe it was too much for them after all," she suggested, wishing she'd saved some of her money for the game machines. "Maybe once Mother Margaret Aloysius realized she was surrounded by chips and videos they had to take her home."

"It's more likely that Sister Germaine had a

delayed reaction to the Reverend Mother's driving," said Sara. "Maybe they took her to the hospital tent suffering from shock."

"No matter what, they wouldn't just go off and leave us," argued Isobel. "And they wouldn't leave the stall."

"I don't think they did leave us," said Sara. "I think we're in the wrong place."

Helen continued to stare blindly at the crowd around the video games. "Perhaps this wasn't such a good idea after all," she said slowly. "I know they've been a lot livelier lately, but the Sisters are old. They're not used to this sort of thing."

"Helen's right," said Sara. "They're used to a very quiet, simple, peaceful life…"

"Maybe we should find the information tent," suggested Isobel. "In case they really couldn't take it and did go home. Maybe they left a message for us."

Helen wasn't really listening. A roar like a football cheer was rising from the video arcade. The boys gathered round one of the machines were shaking their fists in the air. They were jumping up and down so much that Helen was able to see the player bent in concentration over the machine.

"Mother Margaret Aloysius!" squealed Helen. She grabbed Sara and Isobel by the arm and dragged them through the crowd. "Mother Margaret Aloysius!"

Sister Francis stepped in front of them as they reached the Reverend Mother. "Shhh!" she warned. "You'll put her off her game."

"But what happened to our stall?" hissed Sara. "What have you done with everything?"

"Sold it," said Sister Germaine, coming up behind them with a tray of hamburgers and chips.

"Every last thing," added Sister Simon. She was carrying the drinks.

There was another explosion of beeps and bleeps and a flash of black as Mother Margaret Aloysius leapt in the air, shaking her fists. "I did it!" she announced proudly. "Top score! I get my name on the machine!"

Sister Vincent marched back and forth across the living-room, stopping every few minutes to look out of the window. She had never felt so useless before, or such a sense of failure. Not only had she failed to save the convent, but unless the Reverend Mother had discovered the bike after all and had kept her behind as a punishment, Sister Vincent had alienated everyone so much that they'd lied to her just to get away. As the truck had disappeared up the road, Sister Vincent had remembered Major Irving say that he never saw the girls from St Agnes at the county show. She couldn't believe it at first. Mother Margaret Aloysius had told an untruth! "I knew I should have gone with them," she was saying as she turned sharply on her heel and went back the way she'd just come. "I should have insisted. It doesn't matter that they didn't want me with them, I should never have let the Reverend Mother drive by herself."

She stopped to look out of the window. Night had fallen. Sister Vincent could see a few bats circling in the moonlight, but no sign of the truck and the rest of the convent. Sister Vincent stared up at the sky. "I know You don't need to be told this," she said, "but they have been gone for hours and hours. Surely this couldn't have been part of Your plan, to worry me sick?" Sister Vincent and the Lord had been discussing what His plan might be for most of the day, but so far it had been a largely one-sided conversation.

Light twinkled off a distant planet.

"Well, of course I'm worried," said Sister Vincent. "I know that this is just a temporary assignment where there's nothing for me to do and no one wants me to do it anyway, that's very clear, but that's not the point, is it? Anything might have happened. The Reverend Mother's been ill and under a strain ... and the Sisters aren't used to much activity ... and the truck may have broken down ... or they may have had an accident ... or one of the girls might have got lost ... and if Helen's eaten too many sweets..."

Sister Vincent paused, waiting for some response.

And then she heard it. A voice. Voices. Voices singing "Roll Out the Barrels" at top volume above the engine of an old van. She squinted into the night. The Gunga Din Duck Farm truck was just hurtling past the house.

"Does this mean I'm finally going to find out what's been going on?" asked Sister Vincent. She turned quickly, intending to be out in the courtyard before the truck stopped. She tripped over the electric lead, pulling the plug from the socket with a snap and landing on the floor with a cry of pain.

The light went out.

Sister Vincent grabbed her ankle. "Does that mean I'm not going to discover anything tonight?" she asked.

RIDE ON, SISTER VINCENT!

Sister Vincent glanced at the three empty places beside her. Sara, Helen and Isobel had got a lift into town with Major Irving to go to the cinema and the table seemed strangely empty without them. She had an almost uncontrollable urge to tell Helen to stop talking with her mouth full, even though Helen wasn't there. Well, you'd better get used to eating without them, Sister Vincent told herself sternly. The way things are going, you aren't likely to be here much longer. She forced herself back to the conversation going on around her.

"Ten more applications today," Sister Germaine was saying happily. "Can you believe it? That's more in one day than we've had in the last four years!"

Mother Margaret Aloysius tapped on her water glass with her spoon. "Innovation," she said. "Innovation, creativity and originality. That's the key." She leaned forward. "It's as I told the Bishop, we are not intending to compete with computers and swimming pools; we are intending to offer something no one else does."

"Practical but imaginative art courses," said Sister Simon.

"Environmental studies with an emphasis on the uses of herbs and plants," said Sister Francis.

"African motifs in contemporary textile design," said Sister Germaine.

Mother Margaret Aloysius tapped her glass again. "Let's not forget music appreciation and instruction in jazz drumming," she added.

Sister Vincent silently chewed her groundnut stew, trying to look politely interested. This was the first night she'd been able to hobble to the table for supper since twisting her ankle, but it was not the first time that she'd heard the good news that the school was staying open after all. She didn't know what had happened at the county show, but since then the applications had been flooding in. Lying on the sofa in the living-room, she'd heard the postman bring more and more every day and the excited talk of the others as they came up with ideas for improving the school.

"And did I tell you the Bishop thinks he'll get the Schools Committee round here by the end of the week to see what repairs have to be done on the buildings?"

Sister Vincent had heard this, too. Testing out her ankle this afternoon, Sister Vincent had even been outside the study while Mother Margaret Aloysius was finishing her telephone conversation with the Bishop. What she hadn't heard was one mention of herself. That's how she knew that her days at St Agnes were numbered. Sister Vincent stabbed at a kernel of sweetcorn. She knew that the saving of the school wasn't technically her doing. And she knew it was an immodest thought that neither the Lord nor the Reverend Mother would approve of, but she couldn't help thinking that they owed her a little more than that for all she'd tried to do. "They could at least say thank you," she muttered.

"Pardon me, Sister Vincent? Did you say something?"

Sister Vincent looked up to find Sisters Simon and Germaine gone, Sister Francis clearing the table, and Mother Margaret Aloysius looking at her expectantly. "Me?"

Sister Francis clattered from the room.

Mother Margaret Aloysius got to her feet. "You know," she said, as if Sister Vincent had answered her, "I'm glad you were feeling well enough to join us tonight. I've been wanting to have a little talk with you."

Sister Vincent had stayed on the sofa for as

long as she could, supposedly convalescing but in reality trying to postpone this little talk for as long as possible. She knew it was going to be about her future.

"Me?" she repeated.

"How's your ankle?" asked the Reverend Mother, gliding towards the door. "Shall we go for a stroll?"

"I really don't feel up to it right now," Sister Vincent protested as she followed Mother Margaret Aloysius into the courtyard. "I'm still a little weak."

"Do stop fussing, Sister Vincent," said Mother Margaret Aloysius. She brushed several windsocks aside as she strode ahead. "This won't take long."

That's what I'm afraid of, thought Sister Vincent. Although she hadn't said anything about it, it was obvious that the Reverend Mother had been in the barn the other night, and had discovered the workshop and the motorcycle. *She'll have me on the train back to London before you can say magneto pinion.* The thought of going back to the bustle and excitement of London didn't cheer her up as it would have a few weeks ago. She really was going to miss St Agnes. She was going to miss the way Helen, Isobel and Sara would gather round her while she was working on the bike, talking all the time. She was going to miss sitting in the kitchen with Sister Francis, Sister

Simon and Sister Germaine at night, drinking tea and talking all the time. She was going to miss her arguments with Mother Margaret Aloysius. A small black hen raced past her, its wings flapping. Good glory, she said to herself. I'm even going to miss the chickens. Mother Margaret Aloysius had opened the barn door and was standing to one side, her arm extended as though ushering Sister Vincent in. "After you," she said politely. Sister Vincent stopped before she reached the doorway. "I can explain it all, Reverend Mother," she said quickly. "I really can. I—"

"Sister Vincent, will you please go into the barn?"

She didn't go. "I know you told me not to repair the bike—"

"Sister Vincent—"

"It's just that I did assume that you only meant if it—"

"Now, Sister Vincent!" Mother Margaret Aloysius grabbed her by the shoulder and pushed her through the door.

Everyone was there: Sister Francis, Sister Germaine, Sister Simon, Helen, Isobel and Sara... They were all there, standing like a wall in front of the Black Shadow. They were all smiling at her. The Reverend Mother gave her another little push. "Go on," she urged.

Sister Vincent glanced at her. "But I don't understand."

"You don't have to understand," said Mother Margaret Aloysius. "I've learned that if the Lord puts faith in you, then all you need to do is put faith in Him." This time the push wasn't quite so gentle, considering Sister Vincent's ankle.

As Sister Vincent reached the others, they stepped aside. She let out the long, low whistle she'd learned in L.A. "Good glory!" whispered Sister Vincent, looking from the bike to the beaming faces. "What...? How...?" The Black Shadow had tyres; brand new tyres. It had a brand new license plate as well: VIN123. A miniature windsock of white stars on a dark blue background hung from one handle. A tiny ceramic motorcycle had been fixed to the front of the sidecar like a hood ornament. The bike and sidecar had been polished till they shone.

"The Lord gave it to us," said the Reverend Mother. "He must have wanted us to use it, don't you think?"

Sister Vincent turned to her. "But—"

"I don't want you to think that this means I approve of you consistently disobeying me, Sister Vincent." Mother Margaret Aloysius put a hand on her shoulder. "But it did occur to me that if the school is going to stay open after all, we'll need some form of transport until we can raise the money for a van, won't we?"

Sister Vincent stared at the hand on her shoulder, more confused than ever.

"And of course, you'll also be able to use it in your classes."

"My classes?" asked Sister Vincent. "But I don't teach art or environmental studies."

Sara and Helen started to laugh.

"Of course you don't," said Isobel. "You teach motor mechanics."

Sister Vincent looked at Mother Margaret.

"The Bishop was most impressed by that," said the Reverend Mother. "He thinks motor mechanics for girls is very progressive."

"I don't think I've ever seen a nun on a motor-cycle before," said Sister Germaine.

"You're not the only one," said Sister Simon. They both continued to stare at the centre of the courtyard, where Sister Vincent straddled the Black Shadow, light shimmering off its deep-black body and mirror-bright chrome. Sister Vincent was wearing the second-hand motorcycle jacket for which Sister Simon had traded a purple calf. On the back it said RIDE ON. Her wimple was tilting and there was a smear of grease on her cheek.

Mother Margaret Aloysius sat beside her in the sidecar, a bright red helmet over her head. "Now remember," Mother Margaret Aloysius was saying, "we take no short cuts, we stay in the slow lane, and we do not go over twenty miles an hour. Is that clear, Sister Vincent?" Sister Vincent nodded, pulling her own helmet over her head.

Helen, Sara and Isobel were nearly dancing with excitement. "Start it up," they begged. "The rest of us want to have a go, too."

Sister Vincent glanced at the sky and then, holding her breath, started it up.

The engine kicked over on the first try.